I0589673

A Nereid for the Titan

TITANS, Volume 1
Sotia Lazu

Published by Acelette Press, 2018

This is a work of fiction. Names, characters, businesses, places, events, locales, and incidents are either the products of the author's imagination or used in a fictitious manner. Any resemblance to actual persons, living or dead, or actual events is purely coincidental.

Table of Contents

CONTENTS

PROLOGUE

Prometheus heard the thunderstorm that carried the chariot of the self-professed Father of Gods. Zeus was closing in.

Where was Pherusa?

She promised to meet him here at dusk. They couldn't hide from Zeus on land, but her father had Poseidon's ear and convinced him to offer them asylum underwater.

He looked around, though she wouldn't come to him from the land. The shore was empty as far as the eye could see.

They had to go now. Why wasn't she here?

Something glimmered in the darkness ahead, making the reflection of the moon ripple on the still waters.

"Pherusa?" Prometheus tried to keep his voice low, but hope and relief made it waver. He waded into the sea, toward her, ignoring the cold. He couldn't will himself to blink across the distance, since using his powers would catch Zeus' attention, but he didn't have to swim there, either. The motion he'd seen wasn't that far out, and even at this fraction of his full height, he was easily as tall as two human males.

Thinking of humans wrapped him in a veil of sadness. He and Epimetheus had such hopes for their creation. They'd teach them love and trust and honor and empathy. Now Prometheus' twin was dead, destroyed before his eyes by

Kronos, and the humans had been used both to feed the Olympians' power and as meat shields in the gods' fight against the Titans.

Or rather, against Kronos. So many of the Titans refused to take Kronos' side, yet with him defeated, Zeus turned against them all. One after the other, he'd found them and sent them to the depths of Tartarus, while he'd left the Titanesses finish their lives as mortals.

Prometheus had watched from afar, hidden from Zeus, while his beloved Klymene grew old and perished. Tens of thousands of years had passed, yet he still remembered every line etched in her beautiful face.

He'd buried her and run from the Olympian, mourning his lost love. For eons he had nothing to live for, yet he persevered, unwilling to let Zeus beat him.

Until he met Pherusa—a Nereid as beautiful as Aphrodite herself.

Now he didn't want to run anymore. He ached to build a life with his Siren. A life that would begin tonight.

Where was his love? The water reached his waist now, but her head hadn't broken the surface.

"Pherusa?" he called out, a little more loudly this time.

Her tail sliced the water ahead of him. In the darkness, it seemed more gray than green. His little nymph wanted to play. Despite the direness of their situation, he found himself smiling. She was perfect, and would be all his tonight. Forever. With the approval of the god of the sea, he and Pherusa would be happy and safe together, beyond Zeus' reach. Poseidon was known for being territorial; even Zeus wouldn't dare attack someone his brother had granted asylum to.

Bubbles fizzled in front of him, and Prometheus plunged both hands in the water, meaning to close his palms around his Nereid's supple curves.

Something burned his wrists, and he pulled his hands up with a wince, to see a golden rope wound around them, searing the skin it touched.

Zeus' lightning whip.

Prometheus used his superhuman strength, trying to separate his wrists. To break free of his bonds. His hands could move mountains, but couldn't break Zeus' hold. All he got for his troubles was the smell of charred flesh, as the binds dug deeper. He lifted his arms over his head and roared his frustration—not that he'd been caught, but for Pherusa's betrayal.

She and her father were the only ones who knew Prometheus would be here tonight. She was supposed to take him under. Bring him to her father's underwater kingdom, and mate with him. Instead...

Pain speared his chest, and a bright blue light blinded him.

He didn't have to see, to know. Zeus had pierced him with his lightning.

Prometheus' arms were free now, but he couldn't move them. Or his legs. Or even his tongue, to give Zeus a piece of his mind, when the Olympian ruler floated in front of him.

He was frozen in place, and to add to his plight, his mind wasn't affected by the curse disabling his body.

"I'd take you to Olympus, to decorate my halls, next to Atlas and Hyperion, but I have enough statues there," Zeus said with a smug smirk. "Besides, I heard you wished to live out your long life in the sea, so I'll be magnanimous." His shrewd expression belied his words even before a snap of his fingers sent Prometheus tumbling into the black, cold waters.

It felt like an eternity before Prometheus' back hit the bottom of the sea, but his fall didn't end there. The ground shifted, sucking him into a crater, and earth covered his still form.

He wasn't doomed to Tartarus. He was buried alive, while inside he raged against the god who trapped him and the Nereid who betrayed him.

CHAPTER ONE

Three thousand years since Pherusa lost the only male she ever loved, yet the way Prometheus looked when she first laid eyes on him was emblazoned into her memory.

He'd come to her father's kingdom, Vythos, to request asylum, and Pherusa was instantly smitten with his coal-black eyes that shone gold when he met her gaze.

Easily half a meter taller than Father, who was the tallest male she'd seen till then, he swam toward her with his dark mane swirling around his head. The humans' sense of propriety hadn't spread to Vythos yet, and he'd been naked and glorious. His body could have been chiseled into granite, from his wide chest, to his hard abs and strong legs.

But something else had caught Pherusa's hungry gaze.

Vythos didn't yet have the air bubbles that allowed her family and the merpeople to assume their human form, and while Pherusa had often visited the surface with her sisters, she'd never seen a disrobed human male. She was mesmerized by what hung from the thatch of hair between the Titan's legs.

Prometheus had caught her looking and smiled, and it was like dawn itself had forced its way into the bottom of the Mediterranean Sea and warmed her heart.

"Are you all right?" Palaemon asked, snapping her back to the present.

Father and the sea hag hid Vythos in the deepest region of the Mediterranean Sea the very day Prometheus was taken from her, to protect the merpeople from Zeus' wrath, if he decided to punish them for siding with a Titan. Nobody but the witch and sea daimons could travel between it and the surface unassisted since. Instead of a bespelled amulet, like Circe gave Father and Mother for that purpose, Pherusa had been assigned this sea daimon.

"I'm fine. Thank you for bringing me." She managed a smile for her old friend. Not his fault he was another painful reminder of Prometheus' demise.

Not dead. In Tartarus.

Same thing. He was lost to her and to the world, either way. And such a monumental loss it was—not only had her heart gone with him, but humans also suffered the lack of his guidance.

"Do you wish for me to wait?" Palaemon asked, same as every single time he brought her here. His eyes, blue like sapphires, glinted with pity she didn't care to acknowledge.

"No. Come back for me at dawn," she replied, like she always did. She knew what he'd say when he returned too. Not much changed in her life after her hope for a *happily ever after* was snuffed out by Zeus.

May he and Poseidon and the rest of their ilk be lost in Lethe forever. Though the last of the Olympians faded years ago, and she and her family were the only deities remaining in this world, she wouldn't voice her thought aloud.

Palaemon went under with a *splash*, and Pherusa turned toward the beach on which she'd once promised to meet her love. The waterline had receded through the years, and the persistent waves had worn the rocks into sand, but she still felt it as *their* place. Hers and Prometheus', even if he wouldn't set foot on it again.

She slapped the water with her tail, until she was close enough to shore for her scales to give way to smooth skin and her green tail to split into pale legs. She walked the rest of the distance to the sand, and there she dropped to her knees and wept.

Pain, raw and fresh as on the day he was taken from her, tore through her heart and made her stomach heave. It was a physical torment that squeezed her lungs like a vise and stole her breath. Hot tears spilled down her cheeks, until her eyes burned but could produce no more moisture, and her sobs were stolen by the wind.

She sat up and gathered her knees to her chest. The sand was still warm, though the sun had set, but it did nothing for the cold void between her ribs.

"I'm sorry," she whispered to the evening sky, although Prometheus wouldn't hear her. He wasn't up there. His gentle soul was locked up in the underworld, along with those of his brothers. And it was her fault. If she hadn't listened to Father that night, if she hadn't accepted his promise that the Ichthyocentaur Aphros would bring Prometheus to her...

And she was wasting her night, thinking of Prometheus' last day on earth, instead of their time together.

She lay on her back and studied the stars above, searching for a new one. Titans might be condemned to Hell, but there had been whispers in Vythos that the earth itself was nudging them awake. If any one of them could escape Tartarus, it would be Prometheus. He was always so creative and smart. He understood how things—and gods and animals and people— worked, just by looking at them.

And he was good with his hands, too. He'd had a wicked way of bypassing her defenses and making her ask for more. She'd beg him to caress her breasts, her belly, and lower...

Not a moment passed when she didn't begrudge herself the choice to wait until they had her parents' blessing as a couple, before she gave herself to him completely. If she'd done it sooner, she'd have memories of his sculpted body pressed to hers, to keep her warm when loneliness and sorrow chilled her to the bone.

She closed her eyes and spread her legs, for the lapping wave to reach the apex of her thighs.

Prometheus had convinced her to let him taste her *once*. Sadly, the sea foam couldn't come close to the sensations that had made her body tingle. Neither did her hand, when she slid her fingers through her short curls and along her slit. Nothing compared to him, and she'd forever be bereft.

The future looked bleak as her present, so Pherusa once more focused on her past with him.

Father didn't have the power to grant someone asylum within Poseidon's realm, but he'd offered the Titan a secret room, cloaked from the gods by the witch, so he could rest for a few weeks before he resumed running. Pherusa spent her free time trying to spot his hiding place.

Heat spread from her cheeks down to her chest, as she recalled the day she finally found it.

He left the door ajar, disrupting the cloaking spell, and was on his bed, spread legs dangling over the edge. Pherusa watched through the opening as he fisted his hand around the flaccid member between his legs and tugged. She was intrigued by how his phallus grew long and thick with his strokes.

She barely breathed while he tortured himself, his beautiful face contorted in what she later found out was ecstasy. He turned and looked straight at her. "Like what you see, little Siren?" he asked in her head, the way sea creatures communicated underwater.

She liked it so much, she forgot she wasn't supposed to be there. Braveness or stupidity made her push the door open all the way, so he could see her nod.

Prometheus smiled that sinful smile of his and beckoned her closer. "Come inside, and I'll show you more."

She timidly swam a couple meters closer to his bed.

Sitting up with a wicked grin, he opened his mouth and inhaled, filling his lungs with water.

Immortals didn't drown, but Pherusa couldn't think, with his body turning hard again in front of her eyes. "Stop," she screamed in his head.

The oxygen bubble he blew out filled the room, displacing the water so fast, she barely had time to shift her position, so she didn't fall when her tail was replaced by legs. A flick of his wrist, and the door banged shut.

Before Pherusa could blink, he had her very human, very naked body pressed to the slick wood. "I've seen you watching me, little Siren," he said against her cheek. His deep, smooth voice glided over her senses, adding to the ball of fire swirling in her belly. "Are you spying on me for your father, or is it curiosity, driving you?"

She hadn't felt desire this strong before. It took every ounce of willpower, for her to mutter, "My father has nothing to do with this."

Prometheus let out a growl that made her shiver, and crushed his mouth to hers. He ran his tongue along the seam of her lips, and at her gasp, thrust his tongue between them, to battle with hers. His teeth nipped at her mouth, as he swallowed her breaths.

Her body was on fire, and he hadn't even touched her. Yet.

When he broke away from the kiss, she met his gaze. "You said you'd show me."

She cupped her sex now, on their beach, and circled her button with her index and middle fingers, pretending she was with him, in his room, more than three millennia ago, as he directed her hand first to please herself, and then to give him another climax.

She'd been trying to wrap her mind around this new power she'd discovered—to drive a Titan over the edge with just one hand—when he'd pushed her back onto the bed and covered her body with his.

If only she hadn't stopped him...

She moved her fingers faster, pressing down on her clitoris, while she pinched her nipple with her free hand. It wouldn't do. She'd chased after her orgasm before, but without him, it never worked.

Why hadn't she let him inside her body when he asked? She'd let him into her heart and mind and soul in the days that followed, but insisted they should wait for when they were officially mated. Father had given his blessing when she went to him in tears and begged him to ask Poseidon for help. But it was too late.

"Let me see you." Prometheus' words rattled in her brain, as vivid as if they'd been spoken aloud, and she spread her legs wider, in reality and in her fantasy. She stopped touching her mons and grazed her fingernails along her inner thigh, holding her breath as she served herself to the hungry gaze of her imaginary lover.

"So beautiful. And all mine."

She startled when she felt a heavy weight settle on top of her, but she didn't open her eyes. If her imagination offered her one single time with Prometheus, she'd do nothing to make it slip between her fingers.

"Look at me. I need to see your gorgeous eyes." The sea breeze caressing her cheek could be his breath, as if he whispered in her ear.

She shook her head. "If I open them, you'll disappear." It wouldn't be the first time he came to her in a vision, but she hadn't been awake before, and she wouldn't risk reality swooping in and taking him away now.

Something blunt nudged her mound, and in her mind's eye, Prometheus aligned his length with her entrance. "You haunt my dreams," he said. "Why do I love you in my dreams?"

Such a weird question, but Pherusa's body was humming with need, and deciphering a phantom's words would have to wait. "Take me," she whispered. "Please."

Rough fingers dug into her hips, the sensation so vivid, she hitched a surprised breath. Lips, warm and soft, yet demanding, closed over hers and swallowed her moan. When his tongue wedged its way into her mouth, to tangle with her own, Pherusa gasped at the intensity of his kiss. Her fantasy started fraying at the edges, and she tried to return her hand to her clitoris, needing the friction to help her hold on to the tattered images.

"No," Prometheus said. "That's mine." He pressed his thumb to her clitoris and twisted.

"Please," she cried to the heavens, squeezing her eyes shut harder. *"Please."*

His form solidified again behind her eyelids, and she focused on his eyes. She hadn't remembered how striking a gold they were when he called on his powers. She tangled her fingers in his long, dark hair, and the wet tresses felt so real, she half-expected him to be here, above her, if she dared look.

"Are you sure, little Siren?"

Oh, how she'd missed hearing him call her that. She nodded. "Yes. Make me yours."

She didn't expect the sharp jab of pain when he pushed inside her.

Her eyes flew open and teared up at the suddenness and force of the invasion. Her tight sex stretched around his girth as he thrust through her hymen. Her vision was blurry, but she wasn't mistaken. The man pressing her to the sand and plunging into her body was the one she thought she'd lost forever. *"Prometheus,"* she whispered

"Were you expecting someone else?" His smile was as bright as the sun, as he propped himself up on one arm so he could cup her breast with the other. "Play with yourself, little Siren. Like I taught you."

Pherusa didn't care how he was here or for how long. She was finally fully his. She rubbed furiously at her clitoris, while he devoured her mouth and then licked a trail down her throat. "So real," he murmured against her skin. "I can taste you."

He smelled of seawater and darkness and pure masculinity, his power crackling along her skin when he touched her. He closed his lips around her other nipple and sucked, his teeth and his callused hand sending jolts of pleasure to her core in time with his thrusts. Soon, the pain between her legs was muted into a dull throb that gradually gave way to white-hot pleasure.

And still he drove into her, making her writhe and moan, until stars burst behind her eyelids and her limbs trembled with the aftershocks of her release.

His shaft tightened and jerked inside her. He pulled out and pumped his length with his hand, until his spendings coated Pherusa's belly and thighs.

"My love?" She wrapped her arms around his neck, but Prometheus disentangled himself from her grip and stood.

His eyes were wild as he stepped away from her, but his gaze turned icy when he drew it down her body.

She resisted the urge to cover herself.

"Tell Nereus, this was only the beginning," Prometheus said, his mouth twisted in distaste. "Tonight, I took his daughter. Soon, I'll come for his kingdom."

CHAPTER TWO

Pherusa sat up and reached for him. "My love, what are you saying? It's getting cold. Please hold me. Tell me what power returned you to me." Her tone was light, but he heard the slight tremble. What glistened on her eyelids wasn't saltwater; she was tearing up.

He put more distance between them. *Chaos*. This was supposed to make him feel better, not worse. Not the intercourse—that was as incredible as he'd hoped, back when he was truly alive and Pherusa fell asleep in his arms. As amazing as he dreamed it would be, those moments when he slipped into unconsciousness under the bottom of the sea, his mind tired of plotting against her.

He'd believed this to be a fantasy too at first, but being inside her was like coming home. His imagination couldn't summon the sensation of her slick body gripping him, her soft breasts pressed against him, or the taste of her mouth when he plundered it with his tongue.

Should he forget his schemes and take her in his arms? Make love to her again and again until they were too exhausted to move?

No. Claiming her might not have been part of his plan, but it would act as the first step toward settling their score.

"Prometheus, what's wrong?" She gasped and brought her hand to her mouth. "You're not him, if you're scorning me. *You can't be*. He'd never hurt me so. Who are you?"

She'd been the first thing on his mind when the earth shuddered and slid off his body. He'd felt warm blood rush in his veins and instinctively clenched his fists. He could move. He'd dug his way out of his watery grave and propelled himself through the waves, with her on his mind. He couldn't name what led him to *their* cove instead of Vythos, to surface in front of her naked form, spread out on the sand like a feast in his honor.

"Oh, it's me. Have no doubt." Prometheus tried to glare, but her sea-green eyes were filled with pain that tugged at his soul. He hated every traitorous cell in his body, for aching to wrap himself around her and make her feel secure and loved for eternity.

Throughout his imprisonment, he'd planned for the moment he'd cross paths with her again. He expected her to be shocked. Appalled that he'd returned. Scared about what that meant for her safety. She'd try to run, but he'd stop her. He'd never brought himself to fantasize about physically hurting her, but there were more ways to break someone. Like ravaging their kingdom and hurting those they loved. And he'd make her his slave for the rest of time.

Not a sex slave, of course. He'd never force himself on an unwilling female, even if she'd hurt him gravely.

Chaos, had he done so already? Had Pherusa been unwilling when he took her on the beach? She'd begged him to... Was it to placate him? But she'd seemed so happy to see him. And he'd been the first to push through her barrier.

"My love? Please?" Her plea made his knees weak.

What was wrong with him? He wasn't supposed to moon over her. That she welcomed him with open arms and offered herself to him was a pleasant surprise only because it made things easier, not because it allowed him to pretend for a moment that she really loved him.

Plucking her maidenhood should add to his satisfaction. She must have been saving herself for a male Nereus approved of, and Prometheus had destroyed every chance of that. He should be feeling victorious. Instead, he felt colder than when he was covered by tons of earth and water.

Not trusting himself to speak or move without yielding to her pull, he concentrated on the cavern that had been his home, and willed his essence to its entrance. The beach and Pherusa faded from view, to be replaced by a different seaside scape. It took him a heartbeat to recognize it. Trees he'd never laid eyes on cast their shadow on rocks smoothened by the tide, and new structures lined the shore to his right that was much more expansive than it used to be, but his senses marked the place as *his*.

Like Pherusa was his.

He shook away the thought and turned to his cave. Its mouth was littered with odd-shaped objects. Offerings? They were unlike anything he'd seen before. The materials were odd, and the colors brighter than he'd encountered in nature.

He treaded over them, careful not to disturb them and make his presence known, and looked around. Rocks blocked the entrance to the lower level. Hopefully, that meant it remained undisturbed. Not that he'd mind finding a beast had claimed the place as its own. A fight might help fill the void that spread in his gut at the memory of the pain etched on Pherusa's gaze when he left her. He could still hear her cries for him to stay, though he'd put miles between them.

No. He didn't care about her pain. She'd betrayed him. She deserved everything she got.

But she'd remained untouched while he was away.

Unwilling to linger on that, he blinked to the depths of the cave and reached out with his senses, to ensure he was alone.

His eyes had yet to adjust, but he heard no heartbeat or breathing, and smelled nothing but dank, stale air. He waved his fingers and willed light to spill out of them and tear through the darkness. His private space wasn't marred by anything but time.

Not that anyone could tell the space had been occupied before; there was no furniture or clothes. Prometheus shaped the earth to suit his every need as that arose, and he had no need for loincloths, which were an invention of the Olympians. But there, in the corner, the floor was raised in a circle, where he rested his body the last night it was his to rest.

How long since he last slept here?

How long since he last laid eyes on her?

He had no way of tracing the passage of Helios's chariot across the skies while he was in stasis, but it hadn't been long enough for Pherusa's lovely heart-shaped face, sea-green eyes, long golden locks, and full lips, or the curves of her supple body to fade from his memory.

He slammed his fist into the stone wall, and cursed when it gave way instead of hurting him.

"Feeling more manly, now that's out of your system?"

Prometheus spun around at the sound of the male voice, but he was still alone, except for Pherusa's sobs echoing in his head.

"Show yourself, god," he ordered.

"Not until you promise to behave. I saw what you did to that poor Nereid. You broke her heart."

Prometheus' gut twisted. "It was nothing she didn't deserve." Did he still have feelings for her? How, after what she'd done? Her tear-streaked face flashed before his eyes, and he hated himself. For making her hurt. For caring that he did. "And how is what I do any concern of yours?" he asked.

"I'm trying to figure out if you're the man my mother told me you are, or this asshole who fucks women on the sand and leaves them in a crying heap."

Half the words in that sentence meant nothing to Prometheus, but he got the gist of it, and he didn't like how it made his chest constrict. "Avoiding derogatory remarks might be wise, if you wish to ensure your safety." He had to keep talking, to locate the god's position.

"You'll excuse me for not taking advice from you when it comes to manners. I'm not the one who left his woman bawling her eyes out on the beach after he took her virginity." Like a dog with a bone, this one.

Prometheus roared and swung his fists in the air. Not his fault. *Not his woman.*

"Relax, man. I'm here to help, not get my ass handed to me."

What was he talking about? "Why would I want to hand you anything?" And what was an ass?

"I really can help you. Say you won't hurt me."

Prometheus swallowed back his irritation. "I won't unless I'm forced to." Which he probably would be, the way the god was going, and that was a good thing. A god could hurt a Titan, and if Prometheus was in physical pain, he might forget the agony of having his heart torn from his chest by Pherusa.

A male form shimmered into existence in front of Prometheus' eyes. He wasn't one of the Olympians, but that didn't make him a friend.

"I am Eros, the god of love." The god gave him a sweeping bow. "At your service."

Prometheus studied him with narrowed eyes. Could he be Zeus transformed? No. He didn't give off that sense of infinite power. "You're not an Olympian?"

The god shook his head. "My mother was Aphrodite."

That saved him from being pummeled. Aphrodite had won a spot in Prometheus' heart, with her charming, easygoing nature. Prometheus could see the resemblance now. Eros had his

mother's pale-blue eyes, dimpled chin, and golden hair. But—
"She *was*? Did something happen to her?"

Eros' expression fell. "She was the last of the Olympians to fade from existence as the world moved on without them."

The world moved on? The Olympians were gone? So Zeus was gone too? Prometheus wouldn't be able to torture him like he deserved. Fresh fury clawed at his insides, but he stifled it. "Your mother was kind and gracious. I am sorry to hear of her demise. Who rules the world now?"

Eros shrugged. "Technology. Money. Greed. The internet."

"New gods? Were they the ones who freed me? And what about my brothers?"

Leaning back against the cave's wall, Eros said, "You were the first to break stasis. We aren't sure if you were awakened by human action, but whatever caused it, you may want to treat Pherusa better from now on."

"You are here to plead her case?" Prometheus roared. The cave rattled around them, and small rocks came loose to clatter to his feet. Good. He ought to transform to his full size and let the cave collapse. They'd survive it, but it would shut the insolent mini-god up for a while.

"See this?" Eros pointed to a crack on the wall. "This is gonna happen to you, if you're not careful. The way Zeus formed the curse he hit you with, if you were ever free, you'd have to bond with your soulmate, to keep from unraveling."

Prometheus arched his eyebrow. "The words you sling my way hold no meaning."

Eros blew a blond curl out of his eyes. "I was afraid of that. Give me your hand."

The underworld would be turned into a flower garden before Prometheus willingly let a god touch him.

Eros must have known, because in the blink of an eye, he had his palm pressed to Prometheus'.

Prometheus tried to break the contact, but the god said, "Let me show you," and all resistance melted away, as images and sounds and smells flooded Prometheus' senses. He searched the instances for glimpses of Pherusa and hated himself for it, but she was nowhere to be seen. Because this wasn't about her.

Civilizations, rising and falling. Mortals, killing each other and bringing forth new life. Creation and disaster. Nature, yielding and pushing back. New languages. Old passions. New gods—some benevolent, some calling for blood—and humans leaving those behind too. Pain and pleasure and knowledge and idiocy and a million ways of disseminating information.

Also, Eros was more widely known as *Cupid*. Which was Latin. And Prometheus could speak and understand it, along with every language invented since he last walked the earth—including those forgotten.

His head throbbed, as he absorbed millennia of knowledge and experience. *Millennia.*

Eros let go and stepped back. "Now you're all caught up, I need to talk to you about Pherusa."

Prometheus growled and blinked out of there.

He'd been trapped under the seabed for three thousand years, kept from this new, human world.

He'd tried to save it. Now it was time to tame it. And he'd start with the sea.

CHAPTER THREE

It must have been a dream. That, or a cruel joke by a shape-shifting being. But who would do such a thing?

Palaemon and Delphinos could change forms at will, like all sea daimons.

No. Neither Pherusa's old friend nor her sister's mate would lie with her as a joke, and the rest of the daimons wouldn't dare as much as touch her hand without her explicit permission.

The man who'd... *fucked* her, as some of Mother's favorite reads called mating, didn't only look like her Titan, he also felt and smelled like him. His scent lingered in her nostrils. She tasted him when she licked her lips—Prometheus and the saltiness of the tears gliding down her cheeks.

"Tonight, I took his daughter."

Why would he be so cruel? For centuries, Pherusa wished she could have touched him once more. Kissed him once more. And now he came to her and completed her—showed her what true ecstasy meant—only to cast her aside?

It had to be a dream.

Pherusa looked down at herself. The seawater had washed away his spendings and the blood of her maidenhead, but she was sore between her legs, and his palm had left red marks on her breast and hip.

It had been him. Somehow, Prometheus was returned to her. She still felt him inside, and she wanted nothing more than to make it a happy memory, to last her the rest of her eternal existence.

But she couldn't forget his look when he turned her away, or how it shattered the remains of her broken heart.

Prometheus wouldn't hurt her like that. His imprisonment was messing with him.

Why do I love you in my dreams?

Or an unseen power was messing with them both. He might believe he was dreaming too, and that she hadn't truly been there with him.

She stood on shaky legs, to look around. "Prometheus?" she called out. The beach was empty at this hour, but she wouldn't care if someone heard.

She turned one way, then the other, seeking the outline of his body against the city lights in the horizon. "Prometheus, where are you? Talk to me. I love you." But did he still love her? The look he'd given her was one of hatred. And his words...

Soon, I'll come for his kingdom.

He'd coupled with her to prove a point? Something was wrong. The Prometheus she knew and loved had nothing but love for her and respect for her father. Could the ages he spent in Tartarus have warped his mind?

"Prometheus?" she called out again. She'd gladly search for him, naked as the day she was born, but she had no idea where to start. "My love?" Her voice broke, but she kept calling for him until her throat was sore and her eyes burned.

A head appeared in the distance, and then wide shoulders, as an obviously male form slid through the water toward her. Hew heart skipped a bit. Was he back?

The male waved and called her name in a voice she knew well. It wasn't her Titan. Palaemon had arrived, to deliver her back to the palace that hadn't felt like home in forever.

But she still had a couple hours till dawn.

She stood and splashed toward him until the water was as high as her hipbone, then dove under the surface. Her legs gave way to her tail, and she swished it from side to side, propelling herself forward.

She ducked her head in the water, to wash away any signs she'd been crying, and then surfaced to meet Palaemon. "Why are you here?" It came out snappier than she meant for it to.

"Your father sent me. The sea hag said one of the Titans awoke, not far from here, and the palace is on high alert." As the last remnants of the old world, Nereus and his people's survival hinged on keeping their existence secret, and it'd be very difficult to do so if Titans were running loose. Plus Father was worried that, if the Titans returned and found no Olympians to take their wrath out on, they'd redirect it to Vythos.

Was he right? Was that what Prometheus was going to do?

Soon, I'll come for his kingdom.

She placed her hand on Palaemon's shoulder. "Let's go."

Pherusa barely paid any attention to how the waters changed around them, until her father's kingdom spread out beneath them, awash in the pale-golden glow that replaced both the rays of the sun and the moonlight down here.

Palaemon helped her in the bubble and averted his gaze when she regained her human form. "Call me if you need me," he said, as Pherusa was wrapping a seaweed robe around her bare body.

She entered the palace and made her way to her room. She'd say nothing. What happened was between her and Prometheus. She'd shower and lie in her cool sheets and only recall the parts of tonight that made her happy.

Drat. Halie was waiting outside Pherusa's door. For an achingly long moment, Pherusa wanted to slap away the smile that hadn't left Halie's face since she and Delphinos got together.

Shame over her pettiness was added to the swirl of emotions tugging at Pherusa's chest. She should be happy for her younger sister.

She tried to return Halie's smile, but her cheeks hurt, and her eyes stung, and her heart was breaking all over again. "Sister. What brings you here at this time of night?"

Halie buzzed with barely concealed excitement. She always was a ball of energy, but her hazel eyes never shone this bright before she bonded with her sea daimon. "Didn't you hear? One of the Titans is up, and I heard mutterings among the fish that it's"—she lowered her voice—"Prometheus."

Pherusa tried to swallow down the fresh bout of tears, but her throat was clogged with emotion.

Halie grabbed both Pherusa's hands and bounced on the balls of her feet. "This is your chance. You could be with the man you love. Don't you see?"

How did Halie know she still loved him? Halie wasn't born yet when Zeus took him away, and Pherusa'd only mentioned him once, in passing.

"*Pherusa*, I'm telling you your man may be back. This is good news, no matter what Father says."

Pherusa leaned against the wall, letting the cool seep through the thin robe and into her skin, to soothe her nerves. "What *does* Father say?"

Halie flicked her wrist in a dismissive gesture and tucked her red hair behind one ear. "Oh, you know. That any Titan who returned from Tartarus will probably be mad after all this time, and that we should be ready for an attack or something."

The cool was no longer soothing. It felt clammy. Pherusa wanted to shed her robe and her skin and everything Prometheus ever touched. He hadn't made love to her; he'd conquered her. And he planned to do the same to Vythos.

"Father is right," she whispered and forced herself to tell Halie how Prometheus came to her and made her his before spitting out a threat and disappearing.

Halie's expression fell, and her eyes darkened with rage. "That *asshole*," she spat.

Pherusa winced. She didn't recognize the word, but she got its meaning. "For years, I blamed Father for Prometheus' imprisonment. Maybe Prometheus does too." But why take it out on her? Didn't he know she loved him?

"That doesn't excuse his behavior." Halie's scowl deepened. "Though I guess it would explain it. You have to tell Father."

Pherusa felt the blood drain from her head. "I can't—"

"Not about the sex, obviously. About Prometheus' coming after Vythos. We have to be prepared."

How? What could they do against a Titan set on destruction? Maybe the witch knew a spell to hold him in place long enough for Pherusa to talk to him. Pherusa nodded. "Will you come with me?"

Halie pulled her into a hug. "Wild seahorses couldn't stop me."

The contact was more than Pherusa had allowed any of her sisters in a long while. She and Halie were never close, and accepting her support was odd, but she couldn't help feeling grateful as her sister led her to the council room.

Halie knocked, and a servant answered the door.

"We are here to see our father," Halie said.

The man seemed uncomfortable. "King Nereus is meeting with his generals. I will tell him you asked—"

"*Father.*" Halie pushed the door open and strode inside, pulling Pherusa along. "You need to hear this."

The room erupted in objections, but Delphinos was at their side in the blink of an eye. "*Silence*," he yelled, and the other generals quieted down. As the king's son in law, he commanded more respect than when he was only their peer.

Father stood. "I will need a moment alone with my daughters. We will reconvene afterward." Even before he knew what this was about, he prioritized family. How could Pherusa ever suspect this man would jeopardize her happiness by handing her beloved over to Zeus?

"No. They should stay." Pherusa's voice came out a croak. She looked at the seven sea daimons in the room. They needed to hear this. She only wished the witch weren't here. The woman's haggard visage always unnerved her, and her blind eyes seemed focused on her. But Father trusted her, and the witch never steered him wrong.

Pherusa squeezed Halie's hand in a gesture meant to reassure, and then stepped to the middle of the gilded room. "Prometheus is back."

Nereus' smile made her cringe. "He was the one awakened? That is such good news, daughter."

Pherusa shook her head. "He's not who he used to be. He said he's coming for your kingdom, Father," she said loud enough for everyone to hear, though her gaze was locked with her father's.

Shocked gasps filled the air, as Father fell back in his coral throne with a huff. "You must be mistaken. Please, tell me exactly what happened."

Parts of the night were to be hers alone, but she'd share what she could. "Tonight was the anniversary of... his capture. I went to the beach where I was supposed to meet him that night. I don't know where he came from. One moment I was alone, and the next he stood above me—"

He lay on top of her. Thrust into her. Made her come until she couldn't contain more pleasure.

"—and said to tell you he was coming for your kingdom."

Next. He was coming for Vythos next, because first he'd taken her.

Whispers rose around her but were silenced. All gazes were trained to somewhere behind her. She spun to see Prometheus, huge and naked, with wild hair and even wilder eyes.

"Why don't you tell your father the whole truth, little Siren?" he boomed, staring her down.

CHAPTER FOUR

Pherusa blanched and stumbled backward, but Prometheus squelched the voice that told him to run to her and never hurt her again. Only her pride was wounded, for now everyone knew the Titan she'd deceived had found his way between those shapely, pale legs. Nothing like the pain she caused him when he realized the female he planned a life with had sold him out to the Olympians.

But she was so beautiful to look at.

The puffiness around her eyes brought out the green in her irises, and her golden tresses—tangled from their time on the sand—called for him to run his fingers through them. Was she a witch, to still have such a hold over him?

Nereus' seven generals stepped forward, swords and lances at the ready. Prometheus had broken bread with more than a couple of them and would hate to end them, but he would if he had to.

"Stand down," King Nereus called out to them. They lowered their weapons but didn't sheathe them, and their tense posture, shoulders hunched and legs slightly bent, said they were ready to pounce.

Prometheus smirked at Pherusa. "Why don't you tell your father you begged me to—"

"Say no more." Nereus' voice reverberated off the walls. "Though we all know of the fondness between you and my daughter, private matters should be kept private."

Prometheus spared Pherusa a glance he hoped spoke of his disdain, and not of worry that she seemed to use the woman next to her as a support to remain upright. "Funny you and your daughter didn't give privacy a second thought when you told Zeus exactly where to find me."

A squeak came from Pherusa, and when he looked, shock and pain were etched on the widening of her eyes and the roundness of her mouth. Such a good actress, staying true to her role even after all these centuries.

"Save your theatrics, little Siren. You and Nereus were the only ones who knew where I'd be."

"I swear to you, it wasn't us. I loved you with all my heart. How could you not know that?"

Pherusa's cry tore at his heart as much as her use of the past tense did, but he wouldn't allow himself the weakness. He turned back to Nereus, unable to watch the tears rolling down her cheeks. "And you—"

"How dare you?" Nereus closed the distance between them and glowered at Prometheus, impossibly imposing for a man half a meter shorter than him. "I grieved for you like I would for my own blood. My daughter mourned for you every day you were away. She became a recluse. No one has heard her laugh in three thousand years, and you think she'd betray you?"

Something skittered in Prometheus' chest, but he paid it little heed. His rage was too potent, too consuming, for it to allow room for other feelings. "Was it you then, *old friend*?"

Nereus backhanded him.

Prometheus thought he was done being surprised, but this minor deity's laying a hand on a Titan stunned him long enough for Nereus to say, "I understand you need a target for your wrath, but you won't blink into my castle, inside my kingdom, to hurl unfounded accusations and make my daughter weep."

Prometheus should smite the man, but that might not hurt enough. "Oh, you should see how I made her weep on that beach, when I—"

"*Stop*," Pherusa pulled him back from her father. "Look at me. I swear to you, on everything I hold dear, that neither Father nor I had anything to do with your capture."

It took everything he had to withdraw from her warm touch that made his skin tingle. "*My capture?* I was in stasis, buried alive beneath the bottom of the sea, for ages."

"Three thousand years, yesterday. I counted them," she whispered.

Had she? Could he be wrong? Could his imprisonment have cost her as much as it did him? *No.* He'd been the one trapped in darkness. Alone. "You also swore you loved me and would help me hide from Zeus, and I believed you. You think your oaths hold any weight now?"

"It wasn't me. Father was worried that night, and he implored with me to stay here and let Aphros bring you to me. I shouldn't have listened, but I would never knowingly hurt you. You have to believe me." She took a step back, her gaze pleading with him, but it wouldn't work. She'd once convinced him he was her everything. Now, he knew better.

"Every time you open your mouth, more lies come out. No matter. I'm not here for you; I'm here for your father. " To Nereus, he said, "You have a day to hand me your kingdom, before I destroy it."

A sea daimon with green hair, whom Prometheus didn't recognize, stepped up. His hands were bare, but sea daimons could change form at will, so being weaponless made him no less dangerous. "King Nereus, let us detain him. He may be more reasonable after a few hours locked away."

Prometheus laughed. "I was *locked away* longer than you've been alive, little man. See what it did to my reason? Make a move, and I'll show you my true form before I bring this palace down on all of us. I have nothing to lose."

"No blood will be spilled because of me," Nereus said. "But I cannot hand you—"

The old crone behind Nereus put a skeletal arm on the king's shoulder and whispered something in his ear.

He shook his head, never looking away from Prometheus. "Titan, know you are making a mistake. You had nothing but allies in this room until you chose to lose us. I will not yield to your threats, and neither will my kingdom. Make such a demand again, and prepare for war."

Prometheus glanced at Pherusa. Her arms were wrapped around her midriff, and her eyes looked haunted. Her heaving bosom had one perfect breast pushing through the opening of her robes. He'd seen this breast before. Held it in his hand. Nibbled on it. It obviously hadn't been enough, since he couldn't look away from the pale flesh now.

With a lewd smile, he said, "War, huh? Then I guess I'll have to take my spoils and leave."

"Let's not make any rash decisions here. Titan, why don't you put some clothes on, and we'll talk like civilized men?" the daimon said.

Prometheus chuckled. He wouldn't get caught dead in the seaweed robes they all had on. "Like humans, you mean. But we're *not* human, are we?"

Nereus said something, but Prometheus wasn't listening. He wrapped his fingers around Pherusa's wrist and blinked with her to his cave.

CHAPTER FIVE

Why take her, if he hated her?

Pherusa tried to get her eyes to adjust to the sudden darkness.

Prometheus' grasp on her wrist was the only thing holding her upright. She wanted to collapse and sleep, and wake up to a world where her love was back but didn't hate her. Didn't consider her a consolation prize.

A dank scent mingled with that of sea air, and she knew where they were even before Prometheus muttered something and a glow illuminated the inside of his cave. This place belonged to Poseidon's realm since before her time, back when the area was submerged under water, and had been Prometheus' secret home before he asked Father for help.

Prometheus and Pherusa stole moments here together when the scrutiny of the palace was too much, and he'd spent the last couple nights before his capture here. It had been Father's idea, so Poseidon wouldn't realize Prometheus was already living in the palace when Nereus pleaded his case.

Pherusa had tried to locate the cave after he was gone, but he'd always blinked her inside, and she could never find the entrance.

Anger and pain tore her insides to shreds. *Father.* Both times he tried to protect her, he'd failed her and her love. If he hadn't insisted on propriety—if she hadn't listened—Prometheus would have spent the last few millennia by her side. He could have been happy. She would have been complete.

She squeezed the thought into no more than a tiny niggling at the back of her head. The past couldn't change.

She took in Prometheus' chiseled profile. His brow was furrowed, his lips a grim line. But somewhere inside this hurt, angry Titan was the soul of the immortal who braved the gods' wrath, to give humans fire, so they'd protect themselves. Who was creative and smart and funny. Who loved her.

And she should forget he ever existed. Fate had cruelly returned him to her, only to keep him out of her reach.

Pherusa leaned on the cold stone wall and pressed the side of her face to it, not caring about the dirt. Being in here again, this close to him, and feeling his touch set her on fire, and she needed to cool down. To think.

Why did he take her, if he hated her?

"Sit," Prometheus barked, pointing to the raised plateau in the corner.

They'd lain together on the double bed before, while he taught her ways to pleasure both him and herself. He'd held her there, while she slept, on the few nights she managed to stay out of the palace till dawn without one of her sisters coming to look for her at Father's orders.

Now, it was to be her prison.

"Why take me from Vythos? What will you do to me?" She hated how her voice trembled. He'd once loved her. Surely he'd never hurt her.

The memory of his cold gaze when he left her debauched and crying on the sand made no such promise.

Prometheus snorted. "Feed you, for starters. We wouldn't want you to starve. Then... we'll see."

"Feed me?" That didn't sound threatening, unless he meant to feed her to a larger beast. Had she heard him wrong?

He grunted something that sounded like a *yes* and disappeared, taking the light with him.

Pherusa made her way to the makeshift bed, using the wall for guidance. She sat on the edge and dropped her head in her palms. Did he mean to keep her here for as long as he'd been in stasis? *Gods.* At least he'd bring her food. As a Nereid, she wouldn't waste away without nourishment, but she'd weaken. She was only a minor deity; she needed *some* sustenance. And she needed the sea. After a month out of the water, she'd forget who she was and all about Vythos. Would he release her then, with no memory and no way of getting back home?

Light made it to her lids through her fingers, and she looked up to see him frowning. "I don't know where to get you food. There are buildings where there once were orchards. Eros showed me the humans now have"—he moved his lips, like he tasted the word before forming it—"*restaurants*, but I need to make payment for goods and services, and I do not have... moneys."

He looked adorable, fumbling through modern speech, and for a moment, she allowed herself to forget that he hated her. "I can come with you. There should be shops around here. If you cast an illusion to hide"—her gaze fell to his member, half erect as always, and so very big—"your nakedness from the mortals, we can get food, and you can convince them that you paid."

His chuckle was bitter. "You'll have me influence the minds of innocents so easily? I supposed I should expect that, after...?" He trailed off, and Pherusa felt righteous anger shoving aside her guilt and pain, to claw up her throat.

"I. Did *not*. Betray you. Father thought it unsafe for me to come to the surface when Zeus was closing in. He asked Aphros to find you and escort you below. Aphros never returned to Vythos, and we're sure he was the one who told Zeus where you'd be, but it had nothing to do with us." Whether of the land or the sea, centaurs were devious creatures.

"If you knew nothing about that betrayal, then Nereus must have."

"Father swore on his eternity that he played no part in it, and I believe him." Though she still blamed him for trusting Aphros with her secret.

Prometheus closed the distance between them and glowered down at her. "Why else would he keep you in Vythos and send the Ichthyocentaur in your stead?"

"*Ugh.* I just now told you." Pherusa tried to return his glare, but his penis bobbing in front of her face made it hard to focus on her fury that he wouldn't believe her. She hopped to her feet and climbed on the bed on tiptoe, to get as close to eye-level with him as she could, though he still towered over her one meter sixty.

Prometheus huffed, and the intensity of his gaze burned her to the core. "Why should I believe you?" he growled.

She ignored the hardness pushing into her stomach and narrowed her eyes. "Because I have no reason to lie. I'm not asking for mercy; I'm telling you the truth. But you don't care, do you? You've made up your mind, and I'm your prisoner. So what's my punishment?"

He raised his fists, clenched so tight his knuckles were white, and Pherusa flinched. *Her* Prometheus wouldn't hurt her in a million years, but this Titan who wore his face oozed fury, and there was no telling how he'd treat her.

Let him. His touch made her feel alive for the first time in forever. If she were to die, she might as well go by his hand.

Prometheus cupped the back of her head and attacked her mouth with a ferocity that left her breathless. His free hand tore at her robe, until his palm closed over one bare buttock.

Pherusa melted into his touch and let him lead her, until she was pressed between him and the cave's wall. She wrapped her leg around his, trying to climb his body. To feel more of his rough skin on hers. The hairs of his legs scratched her inner thigh, and she tingled at the contact.

Whether he loved or despised her, the passion in his kiss was undeniable. He moaned in her mouth like a starving man offered ambrosia, and she slanted her hips, to rub her center against his leg.

Prometheus growled and used his hold on her bottom to lift her. Her robe got snagged on the stone wall and left her upper back and breasts bare.

He was so big, he was easily pinning her in place with one hand and his thigh. And she wanted more.

She wrapped her legs around his hips and caressed his breastbone, his shoulder, his arm. Every muscle in his body hummed with tension. She wanted to absorb that tension. Absorb the pain of the years they spent apart. Absorb everything negative that darkened his gaze.

Moisture pooled at the apex of her thighs, as his erection slid between them, as hard as the rock he pressed her into.

Pherusa grabbed a fistful of his hair and tugged until his lips left hers and found her neck instead. He sucked on the tender flesh, sending jolts of pleasure straight to her core. She tilted her hips and wedged one hand between them, to position his shaft at her entrance.

He wanted her. He loved her. A bubble of happiness made Pherusa feel weightless. If this was her punishment, she'd survive it.

The tip of his erection brushed against her, but never entered her. Prometheus disentangled himself from her legs, and though he still held her buttock, he let her slide down the wall till her feet were flat on the ground. "No." He shook his head.

"What…?"

He disappeared.

Blasted Titans and their ability to transport around the globe in the blink of an eye.

She screamed, and her frustration bounced off the walls to reach her ears magnified.

Was this how he'd pay her back for what he thought she'd done? Drive her insane with desire and then refuse her?

She used her ripped robe as a sheet on the stone bed and climbed on top of it, then lay in the fetal position. Her body begged for release, her head was light with unquenched desire, and her heart was heavy and aching.

Prometheus was back, but he hated her. He'd only made love to her—*fucked her*—to hurt her. Her eyes burned, but she had no more tears to shed. She curled into a tighter ball and wished Morpheus hadn't faded with the rest of the gods, because she could do with a few hours of dreamless sleep.

CHAPTER SIX

The sun peeked above the horizon, and an orange glow spread across the sky, licking at the mountains in the distance.

Pherusa would look gorgeous in this light. Her pale skin would look golden, and her eyes would shine like precious stones, framed by the spun gold of her hair.

Prometheus roared at the water, and the waves roiled back until the handful of rocks he stood on in the middle of the Aegean turned into a small island for a split second. She thought he meant to… *fuck* her—the word flashed at the forefront of his mind, courtesy of his speed-learning course by Eros—as punishment?

Taking her was foolish. Besides, it wasn't the plan. He was supposed to seize Vythos and enslave her and her family for the rest of eternity. It'd hurt her more than any physical pain he could bring himself to dole out.

"Who goes there?" asked a voice in Turkish. A light shone in Prometheus' eyes, as the rumble of a motor reached his ears. *Nice.* He'd alerted the Turkish coastguard.

He blinked right outside his cave, still shaking with anger. Seeing a group of teens drinking beer around a campfire on *his* beach didn't help his mood. "Leave and never come back," he bellowed, letting compulsion seep into his voice. The kids scattered, and he stomped out the fire with his bare feet. Normal flames couldn't burn him.

But his soul *was* on fire.

Claiming Pherusa last night had been a slip of his focus, and at the moment, he'd been certain she wanted him. Like he was certain moments ago. Only, she didn't. She thought sleeping with him was something she had to endure. Her punishment.

Which shouldn't bother him. For thousands of years, when he fantasized about having her under his control, he dreamed of breaking her and leaving her an empty shell, like he was without her love. He just didn't want to do it this way. The idea of hurting her physically brought bile up his throat. Even in his angriest imaginings, he never saw himself roughing her up— only yelling threats, while she cried and begged him for mercy.

"*Fuck.*" It felt good to scream it. Better when a handholding couple heading toward him turned around and scurried away.

Why did he love terrorizing these random humans but hated the idea of scaring Pherusa even now? After everything?

He'd gone searching for food for her because she hadn't eaten for hours and looked pale and drained. *Not* because he cared. She'd betrayed him, and she meant less than nothing to him now. But then, when she proclaimed her innocence, gaze blazing, he'd almost believed her.

His body obviously had. He'd been unable to resist the fire that burned in him and matched the one in her green eyes. He shouldn't have kissed her, but he'd been helpless in the face of her anger and her desire.

She'd melted like putty in his hands and returned his kiss with a hunger that scared him as much as it spurred him on. He was about to bury himself inside her and was convinced it was what she wanted too, when she'd said those words that sent ice slicing through his veins.

If this is my punishment, I'll survive it.

No. *Tartarus,* no.

What was worse? That she considered him capable of such a thing, or that that her resignation broke his heart all over again?

"Feeling more chatty today?"

Prometheus swung at the direction of the voice.

Eros barely ducked under the fist flying his way. "Woah. You really need an outlet for this aggression. I can hook you up with my personal trainer."

"What do you want?" Prometheus had no patience for the god's antics.

Eros raised both arms, expression serious. "I'm only here to talk. About Pherusa."

"I'd rather punch you." Prometheus tried again, and once more Eros evaded his assault, hopping aside like a mountain goat.

"What is your damage? Just hear me out for two minutes, and then you can go back to your caveman shtick."

Prometheus leaned back against the outer wall of the cavern, the fight sapped out of him. "Nothing you have to say interests me, brat."

"Right. Because you're a cold slab of stone now, and have no feelings, right? My mother used to call you the heart of the Titans. Guess Zeus managed to defeat you after all."

Prometheus growled and lunged for him. And plummeted into the sand, head first.

"Okay. I didn't want to do this, but you left me no choice," Eros said from behind him.

Prometheus propped himself on his arms and tried to roll on his back, but his body wouldn't obey him. "What did you do?" he asked, his jaw clenched so tight it ached.

"It's only temporary. Will fade in a couple minutes." Eros' bare feet appeared in Prometheus' line of sight, and then

Eros sat cross legged in front of him. "So now you have the Nereid of your nightmares. What are you gonna do with her?"

Prometheus kept his mouth shut and tried every single muscle of his body. None moved, but they soon would, and then Eros would share the fate of the Olympians. Or its messier, bloodier version.

Water pooled around Eros, who twirled the fingers of one hand in it. "The waves shouldn't come this far up the beach," he said.

Prometheus' hand trembled, and the water lapped up Eros' calves and thighs. Around them, the wind picked up, spraying them with droplets and sand. "What are you doing?" Prometheus hissed.

Eros moved his lips, but voices rose to drown his out. Were people heading their way?

No. The voices were inside Prometheus' head.

His brothers. They raged and thrashed against their binds. Cursed Zeus. Called for Prometheus to help them.

He had a clear vision of Hyperion in a large room, watching life pass him by and praying to Helios and Selene for release. And Atlas, crouched as if he still supported the world, and surrounded by rubble. The remains of a temple? Was he free?

Atlas' bloodcurdling scream threatened to split Prometheus' head. Not free. Frozen. In stasis. And not the only one.

A deep sense of shame battled the chaos in Prometheus' mind, and spikes of pain pierced him ruthlessly. He should have been searching for Hyperion and Atlas, instead of thinking only of himself and his vengeance.

"Why are you doing this to me?" he asked Eros when the agony subsided enough for him to draw breath.

Eros' blue eyes were filled with sorrow. "It's not me. It's you. You're unraveling." He seemed to want to say more, but he bit his lip.

"And what the fuck does that mean?"

"If you weren't so stubborn and would just listen, we'd have been over this hours ago." He clapped his hands once, and then rubbed them together. "Let's try this again, now that you're more inclined to follow the conversation. Thanks to your nephew, Zeus, once you're awakened from stasis, you only have a limited time frame to find your soulmate and bond with her before you spin out of control. Now, I'm pretty certain Pherusa is your soulmate, which means you don't have to keep looking, but you'd better get a move on, or it's buh-bye universe, before you yourself burst into stardust."

Pherusa, his *soulmate*? And saving the world required bonding with her? The possibility of sinking into her supple body again made Prometheus' heart soar for the briefest of moments, before he squelched away the remnants of his affection for her. "Then you'd better start kissing your loved ones *goodbye*." Because he'd never again love the Nereid who'd wronged him, and if he couldn't have her, the universe might as well burn.

A wave rose like a wall and crashed down on where Eros sat moments ago.

Prometheus climbed to his feet, as a tremor shook the earth.

Pherusa. She was trapped in the cave. If its walls collapsed, she'd be hurt, even if nothing of this world would harm a Nereid gravely.

He focused on her and blinked back inside the cave.

Things were quiet in here, and Pherusa was asleep on his makeshift bed. He waved his fingers and ordered grass blades to brave the barren earth and spread beneath her. He wasn't thinking of her comfort; this corner had the perfect temperature, so he was going to share the space.

He stretched out on his back next to her and folded one arm under his head. The warmth of her body was as alluring as her nakedness, but he wouldn't touch her again. He'd just stay here and study the cave ceiling and wait for creation to run out of time.

CHAPTER SEVEN

Pherusa tried to roll onto her back, but she bumped against something hard.

No. Not something. Someone.

Last night came back to her in vivid detail, as did this morning. Prometheus made love to her, then broke her heart. He accused her of the ultimate betrayal, then took her to his cave.

He kissed her against the wall, before disappearing.

Yet here he was, in bed with her.

His arm came up around her waist, his fingers grazing her breast as he pulled her into the curve of his body. The contact sent a bolt of lust straight to her core and hardened her nipples. If only her body would stop reacting to him... But he'd awoken in her a hunger so potent, she couldn't fathom never having him inside her again.

He bent his legs beneath hers, and if she kept her eyes closed, she could pretend they were lovers, resting before their bodies merged again. She could pretend he loved her.

Though really, *she* should hate *him*. He blamed her, hurt her, and tore her away from her family. And he used her lust for him to manipulate her.

She nudged him on his back and scooted aside, to put some distance between them, but his other arm sneaked between her body and the grass mattress they lay on, and tucked her flush against him. Her head was on his shoulder, her face centimeters from his. She should wake him and tell him to keep his hands to himself—she was done being toyed with—but she didn't know what mood he'd be in, and was in no hurry to engage a Titan who could mold and shape the earth.

So she lay still, her pulse thudding in her ears, and looked up at him through her eyelashes. He frowned, even in his sleep.

Her fingers tingled with the urge to smoothen out the crease between his eyebrows and kiss away the tightness of his mouth.

No. She wasn't his lover; she was his prisoner.

She placed her hand on his chest, meaning to push away. He was warm under her palm, his heart beating as fast as hers. "I don't care if you believe me," she whispered, "but I didn't—wouldn't—betray you." And she'd never stopped loving him.

His eyelids didn't flutter as he covered her hand with his. Did he hear her?

Pherusa let him lead her palm down his torso, thrilling at the sensation of smooth skin breaking into goose bumps under her touch. She reached the line of short hair beneath his navel and circled her fingertips through them. She wanted to follow her hand's path with her lips, but she was too busy watching Prometheus' face for a reaction.

He was expressionless, and she almost withdrew her touch, before he nudged her hand lower.

Perhaps he was reacting in his sleep, starved for someone's touch, after this long in solitude.

She wouldn't be any *someone*.

When she made to withdraw, his grip turned to steel. He wanted this.

Under his guidance, she ran her fingers through the coarse short curls, to wrap them around his manhood.

He was erect and long and thick, and her hand wouldn't encircle his girth, but his hand over hers guided her to twist her grip as she stroked from tip to bottom, like when he'd first taught her to pleasure him.

"Pherusa…" he muttered, his lips barely moving.

"Yes?" She stretched her neck, so her lips were a hairsbreadth from his. Would he kiss her? Did she want him to?

He didn't. His breaths turned shorter, more urgent, as he squeezed his fist over hers, tightening her hold on him on every upstroke.

Pherusa glided her thumb across the tip, and he groaned. He claimed her mouth and she sucked on his tongue in tandem with tugging on his erection.

He was close. She could tell by his panted breath and the way he pumped his hips against her fist. She broke away from the kiss to watch the corded muscles in his neck stretch and the line of his jaw harden, as he approached his release, and then relax as he coated her hand with his seed.

When he opened his eyes, they were wild. Angry. Not glazed in post-orgasmic bliss. "On your back," he rasped.

The ache between her legs begged her to comply, but she held his gaze. "Why?"

"Because I owe you a release, and I don't like debts."

She shook her head, as his words ripped her heart to confetti. He didn't like debts. Bastard. Did he plan on paying her back for every moment he believed she stole from him?

"Suit yourself." He stood too fast, jarring her, and walked to the farthest corner. He twirled his fingers, and water sprung from above, to hit his head and shoulders. Wet like this, he looked like the first time she'd seen him. Only his gaze had lost its playfulness, and his full lips looked incapable of smiling.

She tried to hide her interest, as she stole glances of him showering his large, perfect body. Muscles bulged on his wide shoulders and arms, and rippled on his chest and down his stomach, making her palms tingle with the urge to trace every curve. But it was his long, thick, strong legs she loved the most. She wanted nothing more than to join him under the water jet, straddle his thigh and kiss him, but he wouldn't appreciate her company.

When the water stopped running, he blinked away, thankfully not taking the light with him this time.

Pherusa about had it with the hot-and-cold treatment. What had been done to him was horrible. He believed her responsible, and though she might not have alerted Zeus to his presence, she did feel guilty for not making it her eternity's purpose to find him. She would accept his indifference or even his hate, but she couldn't handle the dissonance between his desire and the cold detachment with which he looked at her.

"*Prometheus?*" she called out. "You need to stop doing this."

He reappeared, holding two brightly colored towels. "These are all I could find in the vicinity." He tossed one to her and wrapped the other around his waist.

Pherusa didn't move, letting the towel fall on her crossed legs.

She'd seen a giant jungle cat on the prowl, one time Father sent her and Galene to the Amazon rain forest, to gather some plants for the sea witch. Prometheus looked every bit as feral and dangerous, as he approached to loom over her. "Cover yourself."

The menace in his voice made her feel small. If only she could disappear as easily as he did. Instead, she made herself stand, put her fists on her hips, and stare at him as fiercely as she could. "Why?"

"Because I won't take kindly to rejection again, if you keep making yourself so readily available."

That stung. "*I'm* readily available? *You*"—she poked his chest—"brought me here against my will. *You* lay next to *me*. *You* used my hand like… like a prop."

He huffed. "I will not be repeating that mistake."

"Why? Because I turned you down? Did that hurt your fragile male ego?" she asked with a sneer.

His icy laugh made her skin crawl. "My ego can take it, Pherusa." Her name dropped from his lips like a curse. "But unless you cover yourself and keep your distance, I'll spread your thighs and fuck you against the nearest surface. Take my pleasure from you and leave you weeping. Again." He spread one palm across her hipbone, his thumb brushing her mons. "Do you want to risk that?"

Her arousal coated her inner thighs. Couldn't he see how her body yielded to him? She bit her lip, to keep from begging him to touch her.

With a wicked grin, Prometheus ran his thumb along her slit. "Do you?"

She held his gaze, one eyebrow arched in challenge, as he replaced his thumb with two fingers, to rub between her sleek folds.

He groaned. "You're so wet."

Only for him. She hadn't been touched by another man in three thousand years. But she wouldn't tell him that.

Her hips jerked forward as he wedged his fingers inside her and pressed his thumb to her clitoris. Losing her composure, she dug her nails in his shoulder.

"So I've been thinking you can't stay cooped up here all the time, and if you want to go for a stroll on the beach, clothes might be good." The male voice came from a ball of light behind Prometheus.

A young man materialized, as if spilling out of the light.

Pherusa squeaked, and Prometheus let go and spun toward the intruder. "You again?" he snarled.

The man—god, judging by his entrance, though not one of the Olympians—held out a palm, his other arm laden with folded clothes. "Don't let me interrupt."

"Too late for that," Prometheus said, as Pherusa asked, bewildered. "Who are you?"

"Eros," Prometheus whispered. "Aphrodite's kid. God of love, and annoying pest who won't leave me alone."

"Sticks and stones... Anyway, I'll just leave these..." Eros looked around and scrunched his nose. "Prometheus, dude, not even a chair? Seriously."

Prometheus flicked his wrist, and a section of wall folded outward, to form a sort of shelf.

"Yeah, okay. That'll do." Eros placed the armful of clothes on there and snapped the fingers of one hand. A flat rectangular thing appeared in his grasp. "This is for money. A credit card in the name *Prometheus Titanas*. Prometheus, if you scroll through the memories I gave you, you'll know what to do with it. It's practically limitless, so you could upgrade your digs too. Maybe buy your lady something pretty."

Prometheus mumbled, "Not my lady," but it sounded halfhearted, and Eros had flickered out anyway.

Pherusa had many, *many* questions about what just happened, but she also had two of Prometheus' fingers inside her, and she'd rather focus on them.

There was a flash of regret in Prometheus' eyes as he pulled away. He went to what Eros had left them, and rummaged through the stack until he pulled out something white with bright flowers painted on it. He balled it up and tossed it to her. "Get dressed. You need to eat something, and a little fresh air might do us both some good."

Food was the furthest thing from her mind, but the moment had passed.

The dress he'd selected for her was cut like the robes they had at the palace, and she easily wrapped it around her body and tied it at the waist. She looked down at her bare feet. "We can't go too far. We have no shoes."

Prometheus fumbled with the button of his short trousers. "There are eateries along the beach." He slid the credit card in his pocket and held out his hand.

She took it. His large palm clasped around her smaller one felt natural. Right. Perfect.

Blackness closed around her, and then the bright early-afternoon sun made her squint. None of the people around paid them any notice, as Prometheus tugged her along. He had to be doing his compulsion thing, planting in their minds the suggestion to look away.

The sand was warm under Pherusa's feet, and the sea called to her. If she broke free, she could have her tail back in no time.

But Prometheus' pull was about more than his hold on her hand. She was drawn to him, body, mind, and soul, and didn't want to leave his side.

As if he read her mind, he said, "If I let go, will you run away?"

"Probably." She bit back a grin when he tangled his fingers through hers. Now they looked like yet another couple strolling along the shore.

Prometheus led her into the first establishment they came upon, a stark-white building with blue tables spread out in a yard under a canopy. He pulled out a chair, and when she sat, made himself comfortable across the table from her, then called the waitress over and asked her for the day's specials, like he'd done this a million times.

"No seafood," he said. "My... companion is allergic."

Pherusa smiled. That was nice of him, not making her see cooked sea creatures.

He ordered for the both of them, and the waitress left. She returned with a glass jug of wine and served Pherusa first.

"Let's see what modern Greeks have done with wine," Prometheus said.

The waitress gave him an odd look, and he laughed. It was his real laugh—the one that made Pherusa's legs weak and her heart speed up. It must have a similar effect on the waitress, who blushed and let her hand linger on his shoulder as she told him to call her if he needed *anything*.

There was something weird about the exchange, and it wasn't the woman's flirtiness. Pherusa figured it out as the waitress walked away. "You speak modern Greek," she said to Prometheus.

He nodded. "Eros gave me a quick lesson on… well… everything I've missed." He brought his glass to his lips and made an appreciative sound. "Delicious."

The word flipped in her belly, and warmth sped through her. She sipped her own wine, but it did nothing to put out the fire Prometheus lit inside her. *Focus, woman.* She met his gaze. "If you've seen everything, then you saw me cry for you. You *know* how I—"

His black eyes hardened, and he turned toward the sea. "He showed me the big picture. Teutonic plates shifting. Populations emigrating. War. Famine. Technological progress. And he taught me a few dozen languages."

"I see." She could think of nothing else to say.

Thankfully the waitress showed up with their salad, along with an incredible thing called *feta* and something like a thick savory cloud with a crunchy crust called a *bread*, and their mouths were too busy for conversation anyway.

Pherusa paced herself until a platter of what was impossibly tasty fried earth apples arrived. Finally full, she sat back and watched Prometheus work his way through the rest of the dishes.

A small smile curved one corner of his lips even as he buried his teeth in a meatball and chewed. He was enjoying this, and for the first time since he was returned to her, he appeared relaxed.

She envied the food for making him so happy, but he might be easier to talk to now. "What do you plan to do with me? Will you keep me on land until I forget Vythos?" She was proud of herself for keeping her voice steady, but honestly, the prospect wasn't as terrifying when he was this close.

Prometheus swallowed the bite in his mouth and shrugged. "I haven't thought that far ahead."

"Then why take me?" She held her breath, waiting for his answer.

He arched an eyebrow and patted his lips with his napkin. "I wanted your father's crown and trident. He wouldn't relinquish them. I thought losing you instead would hurt him more."

She gulped down the rest of her wine, to hide her wince. Its aroma was muted by the bile in her throat, but the burning down her gullet was a welcome distraction.

She'd spent more time than she cared to recall, drifting through one day after the next and pretending to be present in her life, while after nightfall she cried into her pillow for her Titan and what might have been. Now she was no more than a trophy, close to him, and at the same time unable to touch his soul.

CHAPTER EIGHT

He was still in love with Pherusa.

He chewed on the bread that had lost its flavor, and he was in love with her.

He looked at the sun dipping lower on the horizon, and he was in love with her.

He winked at the waitress when he told her everything was delicious, and he was still. In love. With Pherusa.

He might hate the idea of loving her, but he didn't hate *her*, and when her expression fell at his brushoff, he almost blurted out as much.

But no. No matter what was in his heart, his head set the rules for this game, and it said he'd keep her ashore and enjoy her company until she forgot who she was—if there was time for that before he unraveled.

The table between them shook, and her glass trembled in her hand. The waitress hurried to lean against the threshold that lead inside. Silly girl. They were safe from earthquakes out here.

A sound like a hard slap made him turn in his seat. A wave crashed against the short white wall surrounding the yard. Down the beach, people screamed, as the water swelled over the shore and pulled them and their belongings into the sea.

"Is your father doing this?" he asked Pherusa.

Her face was drawn. "No. He wouldn't put humans at risk." She bit her bottom lip. "I... I think it's you. Your eyes are gold, and..." She slid further back in her chair and indicated his hands with a tilt of her head.

Prometheus looked down to see them shaking. He stood and slammed his palms onto the table, making it creak. "*Chaos.* Come." He reached for her, but she pulled back so hard her chair topped over.

"Where?" she asked.

"Back to the cave. Come on."

She took a step toward him, when her name was carried to them by the wind.

"*Pherusa.*" It was a man's voice.

Prometheus spun toward the sea. "It *is* your father. Or someone working for him." He raised his arms, and the waves followed his motion, arching higher than their heads. He couldn't drown a sea deity, and Nereus would assume control of the waters in no time, but Prometheus needed to cause a distraction until he grabbed Pherusa and blinked away.

"Wait," Pherusa yelled. "He's a friend. Let me talk to him, and I give you my word I'll be right back."

Prometheus stood between her and the waves, swallowing the bitter taste of jealousy. Whoever the male was, Pherusa belonged to Prometheus now. "Your word means nothing to me," he spat.

She narrowed her eyes and her nostrils flared. "That is a pity." Before he could stop her, she ran past him and jumped into the water.

Prometheus ordered the waves to toss her back out, but they didn't obey. His hands still trembled, and people still screamed, and now gray slates tore out of the floor beneath his feet and spun wildly before crushing into the restaurant walls and marring their perfect white.

Was he causing this? Was he unraveling, like Eros warned?

His head throbbed, as Atlas' roar bounced inside his mind. Prometheus felt Hyperion mentally slam against the marble he was locked into. Another, primal echo overrode everything, threatening to destroy him with its intensity.

Prometheus took a long breath and focused on letting it out slowly. He wouldn't hear his brothers, because they weren't here. This was his mind, playing tricks on him. His emotions, getting the better of him. He wouldn't be jealous of Pherusa's daimon, because Pherusa was his now, whether she wanted to be or not. He wouldn't be angry at himself for loving her, because love couldn't be reasoned with.

But he *was* still jealous, and he *was* still angry, and he was *still*. Fucking. In love with her.

"*Fuck*," he called out, to the darkening sky. Lovely word. So versatile.

Fuck the daimon and *fuck* Pherusa and *fuck* this entire world. Prometheus would let earth split in half if it came to it. He had nothing to lose.

He strode to the edge of the yard, above a three-meter drop that ended in glistening dark rocks, and tried to make out Pherusa's form in the water. Her green tail broke the surface beside a blue one, and then she was gliding over the waves, hanging onto a dolphin's back. The wind dropped as suddenly as it had picked up, and the beach goers quieted, but they were pointing these… things toward Pherusa. *Cell phones.* And cell phones had cameras that could capture Pherusa's tail and the moment it gave way to legs, and get her and all remaining immortals into trouble.

Prometheus called on the electrons in the atmosphere, and static crackled throughout the air. This would wipe the phones' memories, if he got it right. Humans weren't ready to know about Vythos and its creatures.

Which didn't matter. Because he'd soon be ending creation.

The waitress braved the weather, and in a shaky voice approached him and asked him to pay.

He gave her his credit card and told her to keep a tip of twenty percent—more than her usual, judging by her dazzling smile. When she returned, he flattened the flapping piece of paper she held out to him on his knee, and used the pen she offered to scratch his name on it. He knew how to use a pen, like he knew how to handle himself with the rest of this modern world—thanks to Eros—but it felt fragile and awkward between his fingers, and it snapped in two when he got to the *s* in *Titanas*.

The waitress recoiled, but her smile remained in place. "Thank you." She took the paper back but left him the broken pen. "And this is your receipt." She handed it to him and scurried off to the relative safety of inside.

Prometheus pocketed the card and receipt. It was surreal, this bit of normalcy he'd never before experienced, in the midst of the chaos.

He returned his gaze to the sea, just as the dolphin approached with Pherusa holding onto his back.

It shifted into a blue-haired man, who helped her find her footing on the rocks that lay at the bottom of the outer wall.

Prometheus leaned down and held out a hand for her before he realized he was about to. As soon as Pherusa clasped it, he blinked back to his cave.

He made sure she had her balance, and then conjured a soft glow that resembled that of the evening sun. "You came back."

"I told you I would." She didn't let go of his hand.

"Why didn't you look for me when I was away?" And where did that come from? If he was right all along, she'd wanted him gone. Were her lies getting to him, or did his heart see past his anger and recognize what his mind refused to?

Her red-rimmed eyes pierced holes into his soul. She licked her lips. "I didn't know I could. Zeus told Father you were gone—in Tartarus. I considered taking my life, but even then we wouldn't be together, since death would deliver me to the Elysian Fields." Those deemed *worthy* by Hades were allocated there after their passing, and minor deities had sort of a standing reservation at the place.

Would she have really died for him?

Irrelevant.

He should focus on current matters. "What did the daimon want?" he asked.

Pherusa's shoulders sagged. "Palaemon said two of your brothers are stirring."

The feeling spilling through his veins took a moment to recognize. *Relief.* His brothers would soon join him on earth, and then maybe the world wouldn't have to end, and he wouldn't be alone anymore.

"The sea witch doesn't know which ones"—Pherusa grimaced—"but she's afraid one of them might be Kronos."

Well, fuck.

CHAPTER NINE

Prometheus was quiet for so long, Pherusa wasn't sure he heard her. "What if it *is* him?" she asked.

He absentmindedly caressed her wrist with his thumb, sending a wave of warmth up her arm and across her chest. "What if it is?"

"He might want to pick up where he left off." Kronos had ruled the world before Zeus overthrew him, and had fought hard to remain in control. Pherusa was born after the Titan's reign, but she'd heard horror stories about the Titanomachy—the battle that decided all Titans' fate. "The witch and my father are worried he may come after the remaining deities, to establish his dominion. A war could be devastating for Vythos and the mortal realm alike." The prospect was terrifying. If only she could burrow in the safety of Prometheus' arms...

He had no reason to want to comfort her.

He tightened his grip on her hand for a second, before letting go and stepping away. "Did your daimon friend come to ask you to recruit me on Nereus' behalf?" His eyes blazed in the dim light, and the muscle in his jaw ticked as he clenched his teeth.

"Would it be so bad if he did? You may hate me and Father, but the humans? You created them. You can't tell me you don't care that they'll be sacrificed in the altar of your brother's ego." She snapped her mouth shut before she added *again*.

Prometheus let out a bitter chuckle. "You don't know me anymore, little Siren. Don't act like you do."

She should be more understanding, after what he'd been through, but fury—white hot and all consuming—shoved aside her sympathy and guilt. "I know the man I used to love would never do that." Her voice boomed in the confined space. "I know he was good and fair, and he wouldn't support a murderous, power-mad proto-god, even if he was his own blood."

He shook his head, and tension rolled off him in waves, thick enough it tightened around Pherusa's chest. "I didn't stand by my brother last time, and you saw what it got me. I shared his fate, even after all I did for Zeus. Maybe this time I'll pick the right side."

"*The right side*?" She snorted. "What can possibly be right about Kronos? He was insane before he was ever put in stasis. Can you imagine his state of mind if he's released? He'll wreak havoc. He'll—"

"He'll unravel," Prometheus said in a flat tone. "And the world will follow him into demise."

She couldn't believe what she was hearing. "And you're fine with that?"

He shrugged. "Why not? Eros showed me what humans have done with the life I gave them. They kill each other in the name of religion as easily as they do over petty cash. They pillage and rape and torture. They destroy without second thought. What about them is so special that I should fight my brother to protect them?"

It broke her heart to see him so jaded, as much as it incensed her that he'd given up on all that was good. She tried to reason with him. "What about love? And children? And... and puppies? Yes, there is bad in humans, but there's good in them too. They save each other on a daily basis. They grow and learn and discover and evolve. You cannot support their destruction because they've disappointed you."

"Watch me," he said. His eyes glowed gold, before he squeezed them shut. When he opened them again, they were black like tar, and his face was relaxed. Impassive. "I'm tired. I need to rest. If you wish to go outside and play with your daimon friend—"

"His name is *Palaemon*." It was the second or third time Prometheus referred to him as *your daimon friend*, and it grated on her nerves along with his dismissive attitude. "And if you're implying he and I are anything more than friends, you couldn't be more wrong."

He closed in on her, like a shark circling its prey. "I didn't ask. And I couldn't care less if he bent you over a rock and plowed you, now that I've opened the way. But whatever you do with him, make sure to be outside this cave at dawn, or I'll come looking for you. And if I do, *your daimon friend* will perish."

She slapped him. She didn't realize she was going to, until her palm made hard contact with his cheek. The red mark that blossomed on his skin—bronzed, though the sun hadn't seen him in forever—almost smudged out her ire. *Almost.* "How dare you imply that I..." She huffed. "I mean, that you'd think I'd..." Forming a coherent accusation eluded her, so she raised her hand for another blow.

Prometheus snatched her wrist midair and drove her back with his body so hard, the air whooshed out of her lungs as he pressed her against the wall. "Consider this your final warning. Next time you touch me, I won't stop myself," he whispered in her ear.

He wanted her, despite himself. He'd said so, and his erection against her belly proved it. His breath, hot against her neck, made her shiver in anticipation. She licked her lips, trying to calm her racing pulse. Part of her wanted to touch him and make him lose control, but should she? What good could come out of it? He'd still resent her—possibly more if they made love again.

Sex. It was sex. Better yet, a quick romp, devoid of emotion.

He lifted his head, to look her in the eye. "That's what I thought. So you'd better think twice before laying a hand on me ag—"

She slapped him again.

His stunned expression would be funny, if raw desire didn't singe her senses at the hunger in his gaze. "You—"

"Touched you."

His grin was beautiful and scary, and she shivered when he ducked to tug her earlobe between his teeth. "Then I suppose now is my turn."

It was all the warning she got, before the wall stretched out behind and under her, until she lay on it with her legs dangling off the edge and Prometheus between them.

Her dress had ridden high, and her thighs weren't the only part of her exposed. As a rule, Nereids didn't wear undergarments. Underwear wasn't of much use under the sea, when their legs gave way to a tail, and there was seldom reason to bother with them on their short jaunts ashore.

Prometheus trailed his fingers up her inner thigh, barely making contact. She wanted to scoot closer, rush him to where she needed him the most, but his focus on her face was so intense, he might as well be holding her in place.

He reached her mound and traced her slit with a feather-light caress. "Is this what you want me to touch?"

Gods, yes.

CHAPTER TEN

How could this female, trembling at his slightest touch, have sold him out to Zeus?

The man I used to love, she'd said. Like she didn't anymore.

But she wanted him?

He was giving this too much thought, when her divine pussy dripped against his fingertips like a ripe peach, begging him to bury his teeth in its flesh. No reason to hold back, when she was obviously a willing participant.

But he could make it more about his pleasure than hers.

"No," he said and watched her thighs tense.

She whimpered. "No?"

"Drop down to your knees and take me in your mouth first. Make it good, and I'll reward you." He could tell himself this was about exerting power, but in truth, he ached to see if her desire matched his.

Pherusa covered herself with her dress. Was she going to turn him down?

A smile played on her lips as she slid down from the parapet he'd forged and lifted the hem of his shirt to skate her palms up his chest.

"I said—"

"You said to make it good." She placed an openmouthed kiss over his heart and blew a puff of cool air on it. He'd taught her this, on a starry night, back when there was hope and love in his heart.

No. No... trip down memory lane—yes, that was what they called it. He might not have her heart, but he'd enjoy her body on what few moments like this they had left before he imploded and took this planet with him.

Pherusa kissed down his abs and licked a trail along his hip bone, just above his confining pants, before sinking onto her knees. He wanted to tangle his fingers in her golden locks and push her lower, but every square centimeter of skin her lips touched was on fire, and he enjoyed the exquisite torment.

She undid the button on his shorts and pulled down that metallic contraption called a *zipper*, and cool air caressed his hard cock.

Pherusa took her time, edging her fingers inside his waistband and dragging the garment lower, then scratching her nails down his ass and the backs of his legs.

He pumped his hips, and his shaft tapped her cheek, but she paid it no attention, as she brought her hands around front and scraped them upward, her thumbs digging into the muscles of his thighs.

When she turned her green eyes up at him with undisguised lust, it took all he had not to grab her head and thrust himself between her rosy lips. Still, he raised the ground beneath her shins enough that she was at the perfect height, eye-level with his cock.

Pherusa flicked her tongue over the tip and hummed appreciatively, before stretching her lips around his girth. *Gaia.* She felt incredible, but it was her expression—eager and satisfied, eyelids fluttering—that made him groan.

Prometheus fisted his hands at his sides and focused on remaining still, while she sucked him in, centimeter by agonizing centimeter. With half of his length ensconced in the scorching heat of her mouth, he couldn't refrain from rocking against her, but Pherusa wouldn't be hurried.

Digging the nails of one hand into his ass, she cupped his balls with the other and tugged lightly. So very, *very* slowly, she glided up his shaft until only the head of his cock was still in her mouth, and then circled it with her tongue, before sucking him in again.

Unable to hold back any longer, Prometheus knotted his hands in her hair and used his grip to guide her up and down his cock faster.

She let him dictate the rhythm, slurping at him when he allowed her tongue room to move, and moaning around him as he bottomed out.

Prometheus throbbed with the need for release, and he wouldn't deny himself. His Titan constitution meant he could achieve an erection again seconds after he came, so he wasn't lying when he promised her he'd make it worth her while.

"I'm close." He loosened his hold, so she could pull away, but Pherusa let go of his sack to pump him with her hand while she sucked him harder.

Didn't she hear him? She always stopped at this point.

"Pherusa, I'm going to come," he said through gritted teeth.

She gave him a half-shrug and took him down her throat, as she tugged faster at the base of his shaft.

Prometheus spilled inside her, his skull tingling with the force of his orgasm. His strength sapped out of him with every string of cum that shot out of his cock, and she kept sucking and swallowing. All he was, all he saw, all he felt was bliss.

He shivered and pulled her up by the hair for a fierce kiss.

"Good?" she mumbled against his mouth. She tasted of the sea and the sun and him.

It wasn't good. It was amazing.

He blinked them across the cave, to their bed. He laid her on her back and knelt between her spread thighs. "Your turn." Instead of burying his face in her pussy and feasting on her, like he yearned to, he lifted one leg and placed a chaste kiss over her ankle.

She giggled, and for a split second, the years hadn't gone by. He hadn't been cursed by Zeus. She hadn't broken his heart.

He shook away the nostalgia and nuzzled her calf, grazing the soft skin with his stubble, then licked the underside of her knee.

She tensed. "Higher. Please."

He lifted his head to mock-glower at her. "I am calling the shots, little Siren. You don't tell me what to do."

The perplexed look she gave him couldn't have been faked. "I didn't speak."

"Right." He bit her inner thigh as punishment for lying, and when she *eeped*, laved the spot with his tongue until she moaned and pushed down against him.

"More… Your fingers." There was something odd about her voice.

No echo.

Prometheus glanced up. Her head was thrown back, her eyes closed. He rose on his knees and watched her face as he slid his palm up her thigh and stomach, to where her dress was held in place around her waist.

"Touch me. Touch all of me," she said.

But she *didn't* say it. Her lips didn't move. He'd picked up her thought, like he would if she projected it at him underwater. And yet they were very much on dry land.

Titans could read mortals' minds, but not the thoughts of gods, and Nereids were gods, if minor ones. How was this possible?

He undid her sash and used both palms to uncover her perfect breasts. Her creamy flesh made the perfect contrast against his bronzed skin. He squeezed one breast and watched transfixed, as red marks appeared under the pressure of his fingers, only to fade in a heartbeat. He did it again, and then pinched and twisted her nipple, which rose and hardened under his attentions.

"*Gods*, yes. I love this."

So he did it again, this time closing his mouth around the other nipple and swirling his tongue over it.

Pherusa arched her back, and Prometheus' cock, erect again, demanded to be inside her. But Titan Junior would have to wait.

Prometheus licked his way down the valley between her breasts and grazed his teeth down her stomach, before dipping his tongue into her belly button.

"Hey. That tickles." Her words carried the echo of having been spoken aloud, but the next ones didn't. "Need you. Lower."

He sat back and drove two fingers inside her. "What was that?"

She opened her eyes and bit her lip. "Nothing." But inside his head, she cried, "Yes. More."

Incredible. He tried projecting a thought to her. "Lift your knees to your chest."

Pherusa furrowed her brow, flicking her gaze between his eyes and his lips. "How…?"

This wasn't the time for questions. "Do it," he said.

She complied, and he grasped a buttock in each hand to push her further up before ordering the earth beneath her to raise her so her gorgeous pussy was offered to him as if on a platter. Her juices glistened on the soft curls covering her mound. He sleeked his thumbs along her slit and spread her open, so he could push his tongue inside her. She'd only agreed to this once before, but he never forgot her flavor on his taste buds. She tasted of life.

He trailed his tongue higher, to find the pearl between her folds, and circled it while he slowly edged three fingers inside her. She bucked her hips under his intrusion, and he nibbled on her clitoris, pushing his fingers deeper.

"Not enough. Need…"

He should take his time with her, but her next thought slammed into him with more force than Zeus' lightning bolt.

"Need you. Now."

Prometheus begrudgingly abandoned her clitoris with one last long swipe of his tongue, and stood. He tore his shirt in two, too impatient to take the time to peel it off. His body overrode his mind, demanding he enter her *now*. He closed his fingers around her slender ankles and placed her feet flat on his chest. Then he lifted her hips and slid his cock along her cleft, wetting it in her juices, before thrusting inside her to the hilt.

Pherusa's groans filled the cave as he slammed inside her again and again. "More. Faster," she screamed in his head, incoherent sounds spilling from her lips when he upped the tempo.

He hammered into her until her thoughts reached him fragmented and her legs flopped over his arms and her face was contorted in ecstasy.

When he finally allowed himself to follow her over the edge, he spilled inside her. Not worrying about an unwanted pregnancy was among the perks of bedding a Titan. His seed would only be potent when he willed it to, and this was not the right time to father a child.

Pherusa was putty in his hands, as he cradled her to him, lowered the ground beneath them, and filled it with daisies, so she didn't have to smell the dank earth in her sleep tonight. Then he laid her back down and curled around her outstretched form.

"I still feel you inside me," Pherusa said sleepily. "I like it."

He had to kiss the smile on her lips. "Give me a few, and I can make sure you feel me for a week." His heart clenched. Did they have a week?

She turned in his arms and draped a leg over his. "I'll need more than a few." She yawned and hid her face in the crook of his neck. "I could stay like this forever."

Did she say that or think it?

CHAPTER ELEVEN

Waking up with her bare body pressed against Prometheus' wasn't disorienting this morning. She had an arm flung over his chest and a leg across his hips, and his arm was folded around her waist, his palm cupping her bottom. He was hard again. Or still.

Should she climb on top of him and ride him? Better not while she was sore from last night's romps—plural. Prometheus had woken her up in the middle of the night and made slow, sweet love to her until she couldn't move a muscle.

She withdrew from his embrace, careful not to wake him, and propped herself up on her elbow, to study his face. His expression wasn't tense today, his mouth relaxed in slumber, and no lines creasing his forehead.

Pherusa traced one of his brows with her fingertips, then ran her fingers through his long, black hair. He was gorgeous, and last night he'd been the same man she fell in love with. He'd let go of his anger. He still loved her. He couldn't have looked in her eyes with so much tenderness when he was inside her if he didn't. They could be together for real.

Her happiness was marred by reality splashing across her body like a bucket of ice-cold water.

How could she stay with him, when every day she remained ashore was one day closer to forgetting her past?

Her heart constricted in her chest. Would she choose Prometheus over anything else, even if it meant forever losing her family and the only home she'd ever known? Would she get a choice?

Did it matter?

She trailed one finger down his jaw, then laid her head on his chest, to let his heartbeat soothe her. The love she felt for him hadn't diminished in his absence, and now that he'd claimed her in the name of something other than vengeance, she couldn't fathom ever bedding another male. If she had a soulmate in this world, it had to be Prometheus.

The witch would know. She'd given Father a mating prophecy for each of his fifty daughters, and every Nereid had a century to fulfill hers once her turn was up, or the merpeople of Vythos would be barren for three hundred years.

Pherusa doubted Prometheus would permit her to visit Circe's island and ask if he was Pherusa's destiny. Besides, it wasn't her time. Father hadn't revealed the prophecy that pertained to her, and her next sister to mate was Callianassa—who had a hundred years or so, since Halie'd just bonded with her own mate.

Then again, Circe had given Halie a jagged prophecy that made her seek true love among the mortals, when Delphinos had always been within her grasp. Perhaps she knew something about Pherusa's destiny that she hadn't shared.

Pherusa willed her thoughts back to the present. Her fate wouldn't be decided by the sea witch, but by Pherusa herself. Prometheus held all the power, and if he wanted her, she was his.

She stretched her neck to reach his lips, but a bright light behind her made her roll onto her back and pull her discarded dress over her naked form.

Beside her, Prometheus sat up, not bothering to cover himself. "Eros?" he called out. "You're not welcome. Try again later."

What did Eros want this time?

"There won't be a *later* for much longer, unless you took care of business." Eros' form was transparent, but his voice was loud and clear.

"What business?" Pherusa asked.

Prometheus wrapped an arm around her and gathered her close. "Nothing. Ignore him, and he'll go away."

Eros smirked and leaned against the wall, color filling in his features until the rocks were no longer visible through him. "I wouldn't count on that." He sniffed the air, and his lips stretched into a toothy grin. "The two of you mated."

"No." Prometheus's word snapped through the air like a whip.

Pherusa flinched. "What would you call what we did most of the night?" And why was it important to her that he admit it?

"*Intercourse. Sex. Fucking.* But we didn't mate." He caressed her arm, but his warm touch did nothing for the chill creeping up her spine.

"*Fucking*?" That was what he called the most intimate, soul-baring experience of her life?

"It was *one* of the words I used. I'm only saying we're not mated."

Eros tutted. "The clock is ticking, Titan. Get your shit together, or you know what will happen."

"Don't you threaten me, godling, and get the fuck out of here," Prometheus yelled, and Eros disappeared in yet another ball of light.

Pherusa's jaw hurt with tension. She relaxed it and pierced Prometheus with her gaze. "So last night you *fucked* me?" In her head, she screamed, *again?* How cruel was he, to make her think he'd mellowed toward her—might even start having feelings for her once more—only to destroy her hopes for a second time?

"Don't get hung up on that. It's a word that describes sex. I just meant to explain to Eros that we're not... bonded in some way."

Pherusa stood and pushed her arms into the sleeves of her dress. It was caked with dirt and dead flower petals, but being bare felt more vulnerable than she cared to be. She wrapped the dress around her and tied the sash so tight, she could barely breathe.

Or it was the pain of his casual dismissal that crushed her lungs.

She needed to busy herself with something. Looking at him hurt, but she wouldn't avert her gaze like a coward. The stack of clothes was where Eros had left it—minus what she wore and Prometheus' torn shirt and abandoned shorts—but it didn't look as neat, after Prometheus' rummaging through it. She selected the shirt that lay on the top, shook it out, refolded it, and placed it next to the initial bundle.

"Why did you have to tell Eros anything?" she asked in as uninflected a tone as she could muster. "What did he mean about getting your shit together?"

"I told you, it was nothing. Come back to bed. I need more sleep. Don't you?" He lay back and folded an arm behind his head. When she glanced his way, his eyes were closed.

She returned to her task, folding a too-short skirt in two and placing it over the shirt. She'd let the matter lie, if he wasn't going to be honest with her.

Only it ate her up inside. Garments forgotten, she closed the distance to the bed and glowered down at him. "Tell me the truth."

Prometheus frowned but didn't open his eyes. "I can't."

The knot in her throat tasted like tears, but she wouldn't shed them. She'd cried enough over him. "Then you and I are through. You may keep me here until my memory of the sea world is gone, and you can take my body by force, but I'll no longer willingly share your bed." Every word scratched her throat and burned her tongue, but she'd caught a glimpse of the heavens and would settle for nothing less.

He snatched her wrist and pulled her on top of him before she registered him moving.

"That's no longer your call, little Siren. Now you belong to me."

CHAPTER TWELVE

What was he saying? Making love to Pherusa, sleeping with her tucked snuggly against his body, and waking up next to her had been a revelation. There'd been no speck of resentment in what he gleaned from her thoughts. She'd given herself to him wholly.

But he couldn't tell her of Eros' reveal. For the bonding to work, she should be willing to give Prometheus her heart, and knowing what was at stake would take away her choice.

Besides, however much she wanted him, Pherusa didn't love him any longer. *The man I used to love*, she'd said.

He wouldn't burden her with his unraveling. He'd send her home to her family, and blink himself to the other side of earth—to another planet, even—to make sure she wasn't harmed when he lost control.

Of course he'd have to explain why he gave her her freedom after he'd just declared that he owned her.

He cracked an eyelid and glanced at her face. Her lips were pursed, and her eyes blazed. She looked as fierce as a Titaness—Klymene herself—despite her diminutive stature.

Chaos, he loved her. How did he ever think otherwise?

"Forgive me," he said. "I didn't mean that. I don't see you as a conquest, and I've told you already I'd never force you.

For that, I cannot share why I answered Eros the way I did." He held out a hand, and her expression softened. Would she drop the subject?

Then she curled her hand in a fist and shook her head. "I cannot trust you anymore. Your words don't match your actions, and I won't let you play with my—"

A deafening crash made him jump to his feet. It came from the other end of the cave. He placed his body in front of Pherusa, ready to face any threat, and called out, "Eros? This has gone too far." It could be no one else. Nobody but Prometheus, Pherusa, and the annoying god knew this cave even existed, let alone where it was located.

The sound came again, rattling the rocks around them.

Pherusa touched his shoulder. "Are you doing this?"

He looked at his hands. No tremors. He shook his head. "Whoever this is, you'd better leave while you still can," he bellowed.

When the wall in front of them collapsed, he flinched but stood his ground. He'd pummel the little shit to the ground for this.

It wasn't Eros glaring at him from the other side, though. Nereus hovered there, the long white braids in his hair and beard floating around his head. It took Prometheus a second to realize his cave had somehow opened *inside Vythos*, an invisible wall keeping the water out. Nereus' torso was covered by an armor of pure gold that matched the color of his swishing tail. Flanking him were the two sea daimons Prometheus saw before, Pherusa's *friend* and the green-haired one, garbed in a similar manner, though their breastplates were silver, not gold. Mermen filled the waters behind them, as far as the eye could see, but Prometheus wasn't bothered by Nereus' show of strength.

What bothered him—what cut him to the core and made breathing a chore—was that Pherusa had told her blasted father where Prometheus' inner sanctum could be found.

The withered crone who had the king's ear pushed by the green-haired daimon and hovered to the front, swathed in dark-gray robes. Her eyes were milky white, and her thin, lined lips formed words that never reached Prometheus' ears. He didn't have to know what she was saying, though. She was maintaining the spell that had brought the sea to his front door. If he killed her, would the magic die?

Pherusa wrapped both her arms around one of his. "Please don't attack. Hear father out, and then you can blink us anywhere you'd like."

It was that tiny word—*us*—that kept Prometheus from lunging at those who dared invade his home. "King Nereus, what brings you and your pitiful army to my doorstep?" Hey, he was calm. He didn't have to be polite too.

"I've come for my daughter," Nereus thought at him.

The laws of the sea world apparently applied in their situation, though Prometheus and Pherusa weren't underwater. Was this why Prometheus had heard her thoughts last night? Had the sea witch already started on her magic without them realizing?

"Father, no," Pherusa said loud and clear. She pushed in front of Prometheus, her voice pleading. "He's not holding me against my wishes. I want to be here. With him."

Nereus' narrow-eyed gaze slid from her to Prometheus and back again. "You may still have feelings for who he used to be"—he didn't keep his thought private, but broadcast it for all of them to hear—"but he no longer returns those feelings. Your place is in Vythos, with us."

Palaemon motioned for her to approach, and Prometheus' decision to send her away before he unraveled shattered under the primal urge to protect what was his. "Pherusa stays with me," he roared. He willed his body to grow until his head was a couple centimeters shy from the cave's ceiling. It wasn't his full size, but he was twice as big as any other male in the vicinity, and those tails of theirs were *long*.

"I wish to stay." Pherusa planted her fists on her hips. She could have said she loved him, but this would have to do.

Prometheus folded his arms over his chest, giving Nereus a triumphant look. "You heard the lady. Go."

Palaemon squared his shoulders and looked at Pherusa. "If he's threatening you somehow, you don't have to fear him." Like Nereus, he projected his thought. Why not talk to her privately? Why did they want Prometheus to hear this? Or did the magic not allow their thoughts to reach only a single recipient?

When Pherusa didn't speak, the daimon continued. "He caught us unawares last time, but Delphinos and I can shift into monsters the world hasn't seen in millennia. We can overpower him if need be."

Pfft. The world hadn't seen a full-sized Titan in millennia either.

"Stand down, *boy*. You know nothing of my power. I was here for the creation of the world. I've fought Chaos. I've had"—Prometheus rifled through the knowledge of history Eros bestowed on him, till he found a name for the enormous scaly beasts—"Tyrannosauri Rex as pets. I've survived Zeus. Nothing scares me." Except the possibility of losing Pherusa again, forever.

The sea witch tilted her head, and Prometheus swore her blind eyes saw right through him. A terrible smile stretched her lips, baring rotting teeth, as she pointed at Pherusa.

When the witch opened her mouth to speak, there was no doubt in his mind she'd do something to Pherusa. Unbidden images of his Siren writhing in pain filled his head, even though the crone was supposed to be on Nereus' side and shouldn't wish to endanger a Nereid.

The witch formed a word, and Prometheus' instinct took over.

"*No.*" He shoved Pherusa out of the way.

The witch's cackle came at him from every direction, as Pherusa slammed against the wall and fell.

"*Pherusa.*" He dropped to his knees by her side.

She rolled on her back and blinked slowly at him. "Ouch." One sleeve of her dress was torn, revealing bloody welts on her shoulder, and blood oozed from a wound on her head.

Chaos. Nereids didn't age beyond maturity and couldn't perish by mortal means, but Titans preceded them. He had the power to harm her, and he hadn't reined it in. He'd hurt the woman he loved. Her eyes held no blame, but he couldn't forgive himself. What if he'd done worse than a bump to her head? What if he'd unraveled and ended her?

He should leave, but then she'd think he abandoned her.

The background sounds he'd blocked out when he saw her crumble to the ground rushed back in. Nereus was yelling at the witch to let him get his daughter *now.* Someone growled. Probably the daimons, assuming beastly forms, but Prometheus wouldn't stick around to see what those were.

He gathered Pherusa to his chest, and his heart skipped a beat when she looped her arms around his neck. "Hold on, little Siren." He nuzzled her cheek and blinked them to the last place anyone would think to look for a Titan.

Mount Olympus.

The Pantheon—meaning *All Gods*—at the very top held no remnants of the gods who once convened here. The rocky terrain, high altitude, and steep drops made it virtually uninhabitable, so he and Pherusa ran little danger of being seen as they appeared out of thin air. If a hiker happened to notice, Prometheus could make them forget.

He gently placed Pherusa on the ground and resumed his human size. "Wait here. Your father and his army won't find us for a while. I sense running water nearby. I'll get some to clean your cuts." He could use his powers to bring the water to them, but he needed some time to clear his head. If he'd shoved her aside with more force, he could have lost her for good.

"Don't leave," she muttered. "I'll heal within minutes, anyway. Siren constitution, you know?" Her smile was weak, but it made his heart soar. She didn't begrudge him his mistake. She wanted him close. Could she still love him?

He lay down facing her and tucked a golden lock behind her ear. Her hair was matted with blood, but the wound was already closing.

"In that case, I'm not going anywhere," he said. He didn't mean now. He would claim her, pledge his heart to her, and make the bond work.

"Where are we?" Pherusa asked.

Prometheus indicated the area around them with a sweeping gesture. "This used to be where Zeus held court."

"Really?" She sat up and looked from one side to the other. "His throne room? Right here?"

"Uh huh." He pulled her on top of him, careful not to touch her shoulder, though the skin he glimpsed through the ripped fabric wasn't scratched anymore.

"What would he think of us desecrating it?" She touched her lips to his, and sucked on his tongue when he slid it between them.

Not mad at him anymore, then. Good. He couldn't imagine not having her again, like she'd threatened before her father barged in on them, without unraveling ahead of schedule.

And he shouldn't be thinking of *that* when she was rubbing against his body.

He poured himself into the kiss, gliding his palms up Pherusa's belly to cup her breasts.

Naturally, that was when Eros dropped in on them. Again.

CHAPTER THIRTEEN

"You know, your foreplay is a little too bloody for my tastes, but to each their own." Eros looked down on them reproachfully.

"What is the matter with you, sneaking up on us all the time?" Pherusa glared at him.

Prometheus dropped his hands and growled. "You have the worst sense of timing."

Crossing his arms, Eros tapped his foot on the dirt. The crunching of rocks was disproportionally loud in the quiet. "*I* have the worst sense of timing? You have Nereus' army after you, and you come *here* of all places, for nookie time? Did you at least decide to bond?"

Bond? Like with a soulmate? Pherusa's heart fluttered in her chest. She looked to Prometheus for an explanation, but he let out a disgruntled huff and gripped her by the waist, to lower her to the ground beside him.

"We might, if you left us alone long enough," he said. "Besides, I don't know if she wants to."

Would someone ask her, or was her value ornamental? She opened her mouth to speak up, but Prometheus stood and dusted dirt from his immaculate behind, and her attention diverted to his buttocks.

Eros cleared his throat, and Pherusa snapped her gaze to his face in time to catch him rolling his eyes. "Yeah, she obviously can't stand the sight of you," he said. "You can tell by how the two of you are all over each other whenever I happen by."

Prometheus harrumphed. "*Happen by*? You're constantly nagging at me."

"Why is that?" Pherusa asked.

The males ignored her, staring each other down.

"Well, excuse me, for wanting to protect creation," Eros said.

Prometheus' eyes strayed her way for a split second, before he looked back to the god. "That will not be an issue. I'll leave if it doesn't work."

The bottom of Pherusa's stomach plummeted to her feet. "Go where?" And if *what* didn't work?

The crease between Eros' brows deepened. "No place on Earth is far enough."

"A different planet, then," Prometheus said defiantly. "Another solar system. A random rock in space. I'll unravel there, and this world will have nothing to fear."

Eros studied the ground around his feet. Lightning fast, he picked up a small stone and hurled it at Prometheus's chest.

"What are you doing?" The befuddlement in Prometheus' expression would be funny if his promise to leave the planet hadn't broken Pherusa's sense of humor.

"Trying to snap you out of your self-doubt," Eros said.

Prometheus' eyes widened further. "By annoying me?"

Eros shrugged. "How else?"

"Maybe by leaving us alone? I'd have known by now, if you'd given us half an hour." Prometheus pursed his lips and arched a dark brow. "Make that a couple hours."

Even if Pherusa didn't hate being unable to follow the conversation, she'd be fed up with this posturing. She stepped between the two infuriating males and placed one palm on each man's chest. "Stop, right this minute." She turned to Eros. "You. Explain."

The muscles on Prometheus' chest stretched under her fingers, as if he drew breath to speak.

She snapped her head his way. "And you, don't say a word till he's done." Her skull throbbed at the abrupt movement. It'd be great if they could have this discussion in the sea, where she'd heal faster, but she didn't trust them to remain civil long enough to get there. Plus, Father's forces would be on alert, and she'd rather not have to watch those she loved fight among themselves if she could avoid it.

Eros stepped back and sat, as if on a chair, though there was nothing but thin air supporting him. He crossed his legs and blew a blond curl off his forehead. "Better make yourselves comfortable, kiddies. This is a long story."

"Condense it." Prometheus' dry tone brooked no argument, but with a wiggle of his fingers, he fashioned himself and Pherusa a seat out of the earth and covered it in fresh grass.

"As you wish." Eros steepled his fingers. "When Zeus put the Titans in stasis, he meant for it to be eternal. Mother, Hephaestus, and Hestia insisted that was too cruel, and eventually convinced him to add a clause, so you could be awakened after all the Olympians were gone, but only by your soulmate."

"Awakened, how?" Could her pining for Prometheus have brought him back? Was she his soulmate?

"Technically, their soulmates would have to be within touching distance." Eros' words snuffed Pherusa's hope, but he went on. "I wasn't around at the time, but from what Mother had heard from Zeus—who also didn't witness this for himself— Titans and Titanesses were created in twos, each pair supposed to share a soul."

"That's why Zeus turned the Titanesses human," Prometheus muttered.

So his true mate had died long before Pherusa was born? Sadness spilled in her veins like poison, making every nerve in her body feel raw. It hurt that she and Prometheus weren't two parts of a whole, but what cut her to the core was that he'd lost the one he was destined for. If Pherusa's life had no meaning without him, how did he feel with half his soul torn away?

She reached for his hand and squeezed. "I'm so sorry."

His gaze was startled, rather than pained, when he met hers. "Klymene has been but a memory since—"

Eros snapped his fingers. "*Children.* You're missing the point."

"Stop calling me a *child*, you infant," Prometheus growled. "I'm eternal. You are but a speck in history."

Eros buffed his fingernails on his very short loincloth, blew on them, and studied them, an infuriating smirk in place. "Yet I'm much more relevant than you, old man."

The tension in Prometheus' body warned of violence.

Pherusa cupped his cheek and forced him to look at her. "Let him finish."

"I know what he'll say."

"I don't, and I want to hear it."

The feather-light touch of her thumb on his lips seemed to placate him. His shoulders relaxed, and he clasped her hand so he could lay a kiss on the inside of her palm. "It's your choice," he said against her skin.

But his lips didn't move.

"Where was I? Ah yes." Eros looked extra smug, even for him. "Zeus was wrong, both about what could free you and about soulmates, because..." He made a weird jerky motion with both fists and a rolling sound with his tongue. "Drum roll? Nothing? You're a tough audience."

"Finish," Prometheus barked so loud, a flock of birds behind Eros took flight.

"All right. So working theory is that the oil drills in the Aegean ended your stasis, and the fact that you zeroed in on Pherusa as soon as you were awake indicates she may be your soulmate."

Glee bubbled up inside Pherusa, stealing her breath and threatening to come out in an undignified squeal. If this was true, she could be with Prometheus forever, without giving up Vythos. And with him on their side, Father wouldn't have to fear Kronos' awakening.

Unless Prometheus didn't want her.

Prometheus hung his head, staring at the ground, his expression dark. "How can you think that?"

Her insides tightened. He didn't even consider the possibility she was his soulmate?

"That's not what I'm saying." His voice rolled down the hill and felt as if it came from everywhere at the same time.

"Who are you talking to?" Eros tilted his head at Prometheus.

"Pherusa. I don't know how she can think I don't want her, after everything."

Eros waggled his eyebrows. "She can *think* whatever she pleases."

Prometheus jumped upright and closed in on the god. "Yeah, well, I don't like hearing it."

Huh?

Eros appeared right behind him. "Which may be why she didn't say it," he said, smacking Prometheus upside the head.

Prometheus spun so fast, Pherusa almost missed the moment he closed his hand around Eros' throat. "No more games." His whisper was menacing.

Eros pulled at Prometheus' fingers but couldn't pry off his grip. "All right. I know for a fact Pherusa is your soulmate, and unless the two of you bond by nightfall, you'll unravel."

Fear for Prometheus joined the jumble of happiness, hope, and hurt knotted in Pherusa's stomach. She tugged at the most recent thread. "Unravel?" Like he'd said Kronos would?

Eros gave her a sorrowful look. "His powers will take over, and he'll cause one natural catastrophe after the other, before he self-destructs."

Prometheus knew the danger. Was that why he tried to shoo Eros away? So she wouldn't know he'd bond with her solely to save his precious humans?

The mountain shook beneath them, and dark clouds swarmed the skies above.

"No," Prometheus said. "I'd bond with you because I'm done pretending I hate you."

Hands on hips, she narrowed her eyes at him. "That's a long way from *you and your father betrayed me. Aaargh. I'll punish you.*" Just as long a way from *I love you.* To Eros, she said, "Isn't there another option?" She'd love Prometheus forever, come what may, but she wouldn't bond with him out of self-sacrifice. He'd have to love her back, wholeheartedly.

"The only workaround we've found is for the sea witch to turn him back into stone," Eros croaked.

Pherusa's chest hurt at the thought of losing him again.

"The sea witch? You mean Nereus' crone?" Prometheus asked.

Because *that* was the important thing. *Males.*

Eros winced. "Circe."

"Call her, then. If Pherusa won't be mine, there can be no bonding." Prometheus' eyes had turned golden and blazed like twin fires.

"You'd turn to stone rather than be with me?" Pherusa stood, ordering her legs to stop trembling, though the ground still rippled with tremors.

Prometheus snorted. "I'd mate you where you stand, while he watches"—he clenched his jaw, his gaze unreadable—"but you don't love me."

Was he saying whether they bonded or not was up to her? She closed the distance to the men and placed her hand gently on Prometheus' wrist. "Do *you* love *me*?"

"That's irrelevant." The stubborn fool would return to stasis, rather than say the words?

A boulder behind him was dislodged from the mountain and flung aside by an unseen hand.

By his power.

A strange calm unfurled in her belly, despite the chaos raging around her. "Tell me."

"I do, Chaos damn it. I love you with everything I am." He screamed the words.

In her head.

She could hear his thoughts.

Had he heard hers before? Was that why his responses to Eros made no sense?

She probed his mind and saw his love for her, clear as day—it was bound inside fear and pain, but it shone brighter than Helios himself.

Focusing on where her skin met his, she projected a mental image of herself peeling away the layers of darkness around his heart. "I love you," she thought at him. Aloud, she added, "I never stopped. It's on you that we're not already bonded, because I gave my heart to you the moment we met."

Eros flickered, and then disappeared, Prometheus' grip on him not that confining after all.

Prometheus stumbled but righted himself. "Say that again," he ordered her mentally.

"I love you," she said inside her head and out. "You are my soul. You have my heart."

The earth heaved beneath her, throwing her into his arms, and Eros' disembodied voice said, "You'd better continue this elsewhere. If Circe is right, Kronos is buried inside Olympus, and what you're doing is bringing him closer to consciousness."

CHAPTER FOURTEEN

Even before the echo of Eros' words faded, a splitting headache ripped through Prometheus' skull. This must be how Zeus felt when Athena was born, only no goddess was tearing her way out of Prometheus' head. It was his brothers' screams, clanging against his brain.

He saw Hyperion again, frozen with his arms over his head and at the same time thrashing inside his own body. Atlas, kneeling behind a glass pane, roared so loud, Prometheus grinded his teeth to bite back his own agonized scream.

And once more, Kronos' wrathful bellows overtook everything else.

Prometheus willed the voices and images away. His head grew quiet, but the brewing storm above didn't relent. He brushed a quick kiss over Pherusa's lips and grabbed her hand. "Come on." If it was up to him, Kronos would never walk this earth again.

"Where are we going?" Her cheeks were flushed, and her green eyes shone feverishly with desire. She bit her lip, and Prometheus wanted to bond with her right here, this very moment, even if it brought Kronos back to life.

But this time they'd do things right.

"You love me," he said. He'd never get tired of hearing it.

Her expression turned somber. "With all my heart. Always have."

"And you and your father had nothing to do with Zeus' capturing me." It was a statement, not a question.

She flinched, but her voice was steady as she said, "Nothing whatsoever." She pursed her lips, then added, "I know you can read my mind. Why not see for yourself, if you still doubt my words?"

He was as tempted as he was surprised she'd figured out he could glean her thoughts uninvited, but love came with inherent risks, and he'd have to risk trusting her on this if they were to have a future. "I believe you. Let's go." He realized he was yelling. The wind had picked up and howled in his ears, the air filled with the smell of rain. They were cutting it close.

Pherusa raised her gaze to the darkening sky. "You still haven't told me where."

He grinned. "To Vythos. I need to patch things up with your father, and ask for his and your mother's blessing to become your bonded mate." Not that he wouldn't bond with her anyway, but it would make Pherusa happy to have her parents on her side, so he'd extend this olive branch.

A crack formed on the earth beside them. It was small, but he didn't plan on sticking around till it widened. He tugged on Pherusa's hand and blinked them right outside Nereus and Doris' bedroom. He was surprised not to see a guard outside the door, when a Titan—he—was on the loose.

Maybe the royal couple weren't afraid of him.

The thought pissed him off a little, but mostly it warmed him up inside. They didn't see him as a threat, because they knew deep down he still cared. Like they did.

Pherusa frowned. "Why not the throne room? Or the council room? Father should be there now, regrouping his forces."

"If he's not here, we'll wait. He'll have to go to bed at some point, and I'd rather we talked to him and Doris without dozens of armed mermen vying for my blood."

She tapped his shoulder playfully. "Yeah, because they scared you so much, Mr. I've-had-a-Dinosaur-for-a-Pet."

He snatched her hand and laid it flat over his heart. "Not *any* dinosaur. It was a Tyrannosaurus Rex."

"Sure. Gods forbid it be a *plain* dinosaur." She laughed, but there were thin lines of tension at the outer corners of her eyes. She was stressed about how this would go.

"Before we talk to your parents, I need to apologize to you," he said. "For hurting you."

Her fingers flew to the blood on her head, where the skin had knitted itself back together. "It was a tiny cut. It's healed."

Prometheus shook his head. "Not now. When I first awoke. I would have been gentler, if I knew... I thought you were a dream, and then... I wasn't thinking with my head."

"I forgive you." The words felt like a caress that broke the last of the chains binding him to the past.

He wrapped an arm around her shoulders and rapped the knuckles of his free hand on the door.

Nothing.

He raised his hand to knock again, when Doris' voice reached his ears.

"Come in." The queen sounded tired.

Pherusa turned the door handle and pushed.

Prometheus was close enough behind her to see Doris' eyes light up when her daughter entered. To his relief, Doris didn't scowl when she spotted him.

Doris opened her arms, and Pherusa burrowed into them. "I knew you'd bring her back," Doris said. She had more faith in him than he deserved. A smile blossomed on her young face, making her look so much like Pherusa. She motioned him closer and patted his arm. "You didn't stop loving her." It wasn't a question.

"Yeah, well, he had me fooled for a while." Pherusa sniffed indignantly and stepped out of her mother's embrace, immediately seeking out Prometheus' hand.

He tangled his fingers through hers, letting the contact ground him. "My rage wouldn't let me see straight. Now my head is clear, I know better."

"Good." To Pherusa, Doris said, "Have you told your father yet?"

Pherusa shook her head. "Prometheus thought we should wait for him here."

"Wait? And let him go mad with worry?" Doris tutted and went to an old armoire, made of driftwood and coral, like most of the furniture in the palace. She opened the first drawer, retrieved a small, sculpted horn, and brought it to her lips. No sound reached Prometheus' ears, but Doris nodded to herself and returned the horn to its place. "He'll be here shortly."

She led them to a sofa and two mismatched armchairs, and motioned for them to sit. "He'll be better behaved if he doesn't perceive you as a threat," she told Prometheus. "Though you might want to cover yourself. The palace is not *clothing optional* these days."

Prometheus wasn't embarrassed by his nudity, but he'd come here as a friend and would follow the rules. "I am afraid I have nothing to wear," he said.

Doris left the room and returned shortly with a seaweed robe. "It will be a snug fit, but he'll see you made an effort."

A couple days ago, Prometheus would give up his life before he was forced to put on one of these things. Now he thanked Doris, pulled on the robe, and sat on the sofa, careful to keep it closed over his groin.

Pherusa made herself comfortable next to him, one hand on his thigh.

He hadn't realized he was nervous until a sense of calm spread through him at her touch.

Opposite them, Doris folded her lithe frame in a chair. "So what have you two crazy kids been up to?"

Images from their lovemaking the past couple days flitted through Prometheus' mind, and he ducked his head as if the queen could read them in his eyes.

Pherusa gave him a light squeeze. "Not much. Rediscovering each other."

Doris smirked. "Can't say I blame you."

The main door to the bedroom opened so fast, it slammed against the wall behind it, and Nereus strode in. "You called, my love?" He was still in his fighting gear, though the tail had been replaced by legs. When he saw Prometheus, his hand flew to the hilt of his sword.

"You don't need that," Doris said. "There is no threat here."

Prometheus instinctively half-leaned in front of Pherusa, though her father posed no threat to her. "King Nereus." He stood and gave a small bow, hoping this was enough to show he wasn't here for a fight.

The thin line Nereus' lips formed indicated he didn't see it that way. "Prometheus. Are you here to return my daughter, or to demand my throne again?" His voice was so loud, Prometheus wouldn't be surprised if guards barged in any moment now.

"Neither," he said. "I'm here to do something truly difficult—apologize for not accepting your word to begin with, old friend. I should have believed you and Pherusa. I should have known..."

"And now you do?" Nereus asked. His tone was guarded, but he crossed his arms, no longer poised to attack.

Prometheus nodded. "I wish to ask for your blessing to be mated to your daughter." Out of the corner of his eye, he saw Doris arch an eyebrow. "Yours too, Queen Doris," he added hastily. "As a show of good faith, I promise to side with you, should Kronos arise, and I'll do my best to ensure all other Titans who awaken join us."

Nereus flared his nostrils. "You put us through a lot. My wife has not slept in two nights—"

"Only because of your incessant grumbling and pacing, husband." Doris rolled her eyes. "I never feared he would harm her. Even Circe told you they are soulmates, but you only listen to her when it suits you."

Nereus gave her a dirty look and then glared at Prometheus. "Hurt my daughter, and Zeus' wrath will be nothing compared to what I will do to you."

Prometheus could point out that he was more powerful than the king and his army combined, but he put aside his ego and kept his mouth shut.

"Good boy," Pherusa said in his head.

"You like me better when I'm bad," he replied in the same manner.

Doris glanced from one to the other, then slid her gaze to Nereus and smiled.

Nereus shook his head. "If my wife is correct—"

"Which I always am."

"—you are already mentally linked. Far be it from me to keep my daughter from a happiness long due. You have my blessing. Both of you."

Pherusa's face glowed with happiness. "Mother?"

"Let me think about it." Doris scratched her chin.

"*Mother.*"

"All right, *daughter*. You and your beloved have my blessing. May your eternity be filled with love."

"And sex," Prometheus thought at Pherusa.

Her pale skin turned rosy with the most beautiful blush. "Then, if you'll excuse us, we'll be in my room," she said with a giggle.

Nereus covered his face with his palm. "And I will be far, far away," he mumbled. "The Atlantic is nice, this time of the year."

Prometheus didn't hear what Doris said, because he was too busy blinking Pherusa and himself to her bedroom, on the other side of this floor of the palace.

He took in the room before him. He'd been here a couple of times, in another lifetime, and it hit him hard how unchanged it remained. Time had frozen for the girl—woman—who lived here.

The curved single bed, forged out of pink coral, was adorned with white sheets and a dozen of fluffy pillows, picked up from shipwrecks through the years. Their colors had barely faded, the magical light of Vythos nowhere near as destructive as the rays of the sun.

The nightstands were littered with pieces of colored glass, smoothened by the waves, and shells in all shapes, hues, and sizes. Even the pale golden glow of Vythos was filtered through red-tinted glass, washing the room in pink hues.

A vaguely humanoid shape caught his eye at the far left corner. Was someone else in the room?

He spun, pushing Pherusa behind him, and blinked in disbelief. A statue of himself in bronze stood there, smirking at him. The resemblance was uncanny. He turned to face Pherusa, who was blushing. "How...?"

Her lips twitched. "From memory."

The level of detail was astonishing. "You made this?"

"I had help, but mostly yes. Took me a few hundred tries to get it right. I needed to see you, so I forged you."

How had he ever doubted this woman's loyalty and love? He slanted his mouth over hers and poured everything he felt—his every hope and fear and all his love—into this kiss.

She pushed gently on his chest and whispered against his lips, "We're filthy."

What?

Oh, she meant it literally. Sprigs clung to their hair, her dress was matted with mud, and his ass had a coating of dirt. Shower sex could be fun, but he wanted to bond with her in her bed. "I have an idea," he said.

"What?" she asked in his head.

He blinked them to the ocean, for the water to clean them. Pherusa's legs melded into a gorgeous green tail that she flapped from side to side, as she glared at him. "You could have given me a moment's warning," she thought at him.

Prometheus laughed, not minding the water rushing in his mouth and down his throat. Titans couldn't drown, after all.

"We can't blink back to my room like this. Everything will get wet," she sent him.

The mental image of her divine pussy accompanied her words, and he was painfully hard in a heartbeat. But he'd do things the way his Siren wanted. He focused on the top of the castle, just inside the bubble, and in a split second, they materialized on the soft pillows there. Pherusa stood and discarded her soggy dress, and he took off his robe in favor of a dry one she handed him from beside the door.

"Thetis made sure these are on all of the entrances to the palace, so nobody's sensibilities are offended," she said with a smirk as she wore one too. She twisted the water from her long, golden locks and held the door open. "Shall we?"

CHAPTER FIFTEEN

Pherusa was thankful they ran into none of her siblings or any of the palace staff on their way to her room. Nothing should delay their lovemaking.

The moment her door was closed behind them, though, butterflies fluttered in her stomach. Why was she so nervous?

Perhaps because she'd dreamed of this moment so often but never expected to experience it. Now it seemed her long life had always been leading to this.

Prometheus was about to make love to her in her virginal bed—the same bed in which she'd fantasized about him a million times while she pleasured herself, never reaching the peaks he took her to.

She stood on her tiptoes, to lay a soft kiss on his lips, then held out a hand to him.

He gazed at it reverently, before closing his large palm around hers and letting her lead him to her bed.

Her fingers trembled as she undid the sash of his robe, as if she hadn't touched his body mere hours ago.

He stopped her and tilted her chin up, so she'd meet his eyes. "There is no need to rush this."

Right. Because the world *wasn't* hanging on the balance. She forced a smile that turned real when she saw the laugh lines around his gorgeous black eyes.

"Let me," Prometheus said, and she sat on the bed, waiting for him to undo his robe.

Instead, he gently nudged her to lie back and stretched beside her on her narrow mattress. "Are you sure about this?" he asked.

What? Making love?

He sombered, studying her face. "I understand if you don't want to bind yourself to me for—"

"I do." Did she sound too eager? Who cared? "It's all I want. Please make love to me, my Titan."

His smile was dazzling. He buried his face in the crook of her neck and inhaled deeply. "You smell of home. Of the ocean and the dawn and creation itself."

His new beard tickled her sensitive skin, yet her giggle wasn't a reaction to that but an expression of pure happiness.

Prometheus' agile fingertips found the neckline of her robe and slipped underneath it, to trace the valley between her breasts and skim down to her navel. "I love touching you," he whispered and nibbled on her earlobe. "Your body is so responsive." He undid the belt keeping her robe in place and continued his trail down her belly and then her thigh, uncovering a strip of skin a couple centimeters wide.

Pherusa wanted the stupid robe to disappear, so he could touch more of her.

Prometheus licked along her collar bone and shoved aside the fabric covering one breast. He teased the nipple with his palm, barely touching the sensitive peak that puckered and tingled with the need for more attention. "See how inviting your breasts are? How can I resist?"

"Who says you have to?" she muttered, tangling her fingers in his hair to bring his head lower until he grazed her nipple with his teeth.

The sharp sensation was replaced by the warmth of his mouth, as he closed his lips around the tender flesh and sucked, sending a jolt of pleasure to her womb.

He skated his palm down her stomach, caressed her hipbone, dragged his fingers up her thigh, and kept sucking on her breast.

Pherusa spread her legs, moisture pooling at her core. "Take your time with me later. Now I need you inside me."

He raised his gaze to her face. "I didn't prepare you." His hand slipped between her legs, and his expression turned hungry when he dipped a finger inside. "Seems I don't have to."

She shook her head. "In me. Now."

He laughed as he rolled his body over hers, and kept laughing as he slowly entered her.

It did delightful things to her nether region, but mostly, it made her heart expand. He was relaxed and carefree and with her. Really with her. This coupling held no trace of urgency or resentment. No fear that he'd cast her aside when they were done.

With every thrust of his hips, Prometheus declared his love for her through their mental link. His eyes blazed gold with desire as he drove in and out of her body, pulling tiny mewls and moans from her lips. "Who do you belong to, Pherusa?" he asked, withdrawing until only the tip of his erection remained in her.

Pherusa tilted her hips. "You. I belong to you. My heart is yours." In his head, she added, "Forever."

Prometheus tensed, every muscle in his body coiled. He squeezed his eyes shut and shook his head, his expression pained.

Was he having second thoughts?

"Never." His answer rang in her head, and he opened his eyes again, to look at her with a near-tangible intensity. He inched back inside so agonizingly slowly, she buried her nails in his wide shoulders and pushed her heels into his buttocks. When he was seated all the way inside, he said, "My heart is yours. Forever."

Nothing snapped in place. No supernatural string sprung between them. But Pherusa knew the bonding was successful, because of the sense of completeness that spread throughout her body. She was where she was meant to be.

With Prometheus. Forever.

She caressed his mind with her thoughts and was filled with wonder. Even now, he was amazed she was his.

She pumped her hips and urged him on. They'd done their service to the world. Now they were going to have fun.

Prometheus gave her a feral grin and dug his fingers in her hips. He knelt on one leg, the other planted firmly on the floor, the adjusted position both changing the angle of his strokes and adding to his momentum.

Her body bowed the way he held her hips, Pherusa's pulse thudded in her ears as he drove inside her in a steady, measured tempo, stoking the ball of fire in her belly. Her head was light. She tried to bring her hand to her mound, to touch her clitoris and add the friction she needed to orgasm, but her limbs wouldn't follow orders. "Need..."

Without slowing his thrusts, Prometheus splayed his hand over her belly and dragged it down her body, to where they were joined. "I love seeing you like this, wild and ravenous for me." He drew his thumb along her lower lips and to her clitoris, to circle the sensitive button in ever tightening loops. As he added pressure to his touch, he slammed inside her harder, without changing his rhythm. He kept her on a plateau of pleasure, not letting her fall over the edge.

"Say *please*." He pinched her clitoris between index and middle finger, making her groan.

"Please. *Now.*"

Her eyelids were heavy, but she kept them open long enough to see his satisfied smirk, as he thrust inside her in a frantic pace, twisting his thumb on her clitoris. The combination of sensations made her feel like she was the one unraveling, pleasure splitting her open for the fire inside to consume the world.

Prometheus kept pistoning into her, until he reached completion with a roar that made the room shake and a fresh rush of heat spread up her neck to her cheeks. Everyone in the palace must have heard that.

She tugged on his hand and used her tongue to lick his fingers clean, feeling him harden inside her once more.

Pherusa was sated and pleasantly sore, and wouldn't say *no* to a couple hours of sleep, but when Prometheus waggled his eyebrows, she decided rest could wait.

Eros obviously couldn't.

She saw his head appear behind Prometheus' shoulder.

"About time, people," he said and clapped his hands.

"This time, I'll fucking kill him," Prometheus roared. He blinked behind the god and was fast enough to get him in a choke hold. Prometheus' gaze zeroed in to between Pherusa's legs, and he scowled.

Gods, she was exposed for Eros to look his fill. Nereids weren't inherently shy, but this was a private moment, and Eros was intruding. She crossed her legs and scooted higher on the bed, covering herself with her robe.

"Speak your piece and take your chances, godling," Prometheus growled.

"You're not the thankful sort, are you?" Eros harrumphed. "I'm here to congratulate you on your bonding and let you know Hyperion is up and running. Naked. In a hotel somewhere."

Prometheus adjusted his grip, glaring daggers at Eros. "Has he found his mate?"

"She's who he's running after," Eros said with an exaggerated sigh. "Let's just say he'll need less prompting than you did."

Looking at Pherusa, Prometheus said, "I should go to him. Help him—"

"You'll do no such thing." Eros' voice was so amplified, Pherusa winced and covered her ears, though she still heard what he said next. "Unbonded Titans are unstable, and the proximity of their siblings can exacerbate their unraveling. I'll bring him to you when it's safe."

CHAPTER SIXTEEN

Bring Hyperion where, though? Would Prometheus and Pherusa live in the palace?

She must have read his mind, because she said, "I'd be as happy in your cave as I'd be here, as long as I'm with you."

Could he possibly love her more?

Eros *aww*'ed. "That's adorable, but Big Guy can afford a mansion to house your love now. The credit card I gave him?"

Prometheus nodded. It was in the pocket of his shorts, somewhere on the floor of his cave.

Eros went on. "I told you it has no limit. It's linked to a rather hefty bank account, and everything else you need is here." He somehow slipped from Prometheus' grasp. When he snapped his fingers, a large brown envelop slapped the floor by Prometheus' feet.

As Prometheus reached for it, the god said, "We'll be in touch," and disappeared in a cloud of sparks.

Prometheus flicked through the envelope. Birth certificate, ID card, driver's license, passport, and a handful more credit cards, as well as a cell phone.

"What's in it?" Pherusa asked.

He tossed the envelope on her dresser and crawled into bed next to her. It was a tight fit, but it'd do till they found the perfect place. "Nothing important," he said. "All that matters is in this bed with me."

She turned in his arms and draped a leg over his, her wet center pressed against his cock. "I believe we were in the middle of something."

He claimed her mouth and pushed inside her slowly, until he was fully sheathed.

Pherusa sighed. "I like this."

"Good, because it's going to be happening a lot." He rocked against her, holding her gaze. "I was thinking we should get a big place. Many bedrooms."

"For visitors?" She bit her lip as he twisted his hips.

"Or children." He watched her face for any signs of distress. They'd never talked about this before, but there was no rush.

The smile that blossomed on her lips made his heart race. "Sounds good."

They made love until Pherusa's eyes drifted shut. He curved his body around hers, without withdrawing from inside her. This was what he wanted for eternity.

He ached to follow her into slumber, but the image that had flashed through his mind the moment of their bonding wouldn't let him. Glimpsing the face he thought he'd never see again had chilled him to the bone. *Epimetheus.* Prometheus believed his twin dead, not trapped. He'd seen him turned to dust by Kronos, before the Titanomachy. Was there hope for him yet?

He touched his lips to Pherusa's temple and watched her sleep. He had his soulmate, and now his brother might be returned to him too. He wouldn't tell her anything, but once they'd settled in a place of their own, he'd talk to Eros. The thought soured in his gut. He hated admitting it, but he already owed the little god more than he was comfortable with.

Call it restitution for what the Olympians had done to him and his brothers.

He kissed the tip of Pherusa's nose and closed his eyes.

He awoke to something pressing down on him. Was he still under the seabed? Had the past couple days been a dream? Panic sliced through him at the thought he was still in stasis. But no, this wasn't cold mud covering his body. It was the supple form of his little Siren.

Prometheus blinked away the last dregs of his sleep and folded his arms under his head. "You feel like going for a ride?" He pumped his hips.

Pherusa wiggled and planted her hands on his shoulders, her face centimeters from his. "I just wanted to take a good look at you." When she sat back, her heat was pressed to his shaft, but she made no effort to take him inside, and he was happy to lie here, gazing into her adoring eyes.

"Talk to me," she said. "What was it like, where you were?"

He rolled back his head and brought his hand to her thigh, to caress the silky skin. "Dark. Wet. Cold. I could feel the pressure and the cold, but nothing else."

She swallowed audibly. "Did you... Were you aware, the entire time?"

Was he? He drew circles with his fingers on her bare back. "I'm not sure. I think I swam in and out of consciousness. Dreamed of you a lot—or it was fantasies. Might have been part of Zeus' curse. Sometimes we had this. Others..." Others, he made her pay for betraying him. He made her cry.

Pherusa sprawled on top of him, her fingers idly playing with the hairs in his armpit. "You were living but dead. Like..." From her mind, he picked up the rest of that thought. "Like me."

His first instinct was to protest the belittling of his ordeal—she'd been at home with her family and friends—but moisture gathered where her cheek lay on his chest. He'd made her cry again.

She pressed her lips to his skin, over his heart. "I breathed and moved freely, but inside, I was in stasis, with you. I drifted through the days, looking forward to bedtime, when I'd hopefully see you in my dreams."

Prometheus wanted to tell her it was all right, that he was here now, but he felt her need to talk about her pain and exorcise the ghost of their forced separation.

"When you... came to me on the beach, I thought my dreams had come true. That my love summoned you."

"It probably did, but I was an asshole and didn't realize it."

She raised her head. Her eyes were red rimmed, but her expression serene. She scrunched her nose. "I don't know the exact meaning of that word."

"A jerk. An idiot. A brute, who hurt you out of his own insecurities."

"Yes. All of that. But you were hurt too. You lost eons of your life. We have so much catching up to do, and I plan on enjoying everything with you, both under the sea and on the surface."

And they could heal. Together.

He *could* love her more, and he did, with every moment that passed. He'd gladly show her again, but a knock on the door reminded him they weren't alone in the palace. "Hold on," he called out. Begrudgingly, he rolled Pherusa off his body. He stooped to snatch their robes from the floor, helped Pherusa with hers, and then pulled on his own.

Pherusa sat primly on the foot of the bed, but her meticulously closed neckline couldn't hide her messy hair, bee stung lips, and flush skin. "What?" she asked when she caught him looking.

"You might as well be wearing a *Thoroughly Debouched* sign around your neck."

He left her maniacally finger-combing her hair, and went to answer the door.

Nerites, Pherusa's only brother, stood outside, a sly smirk on his lips. "You're alive," he said. "We were worried when you missed breakfast."

From behind Prometheus, Pherusa asked, "Is it Eros again?"

Prometheus replied, "As if that little prick would ever knock. No, it's your brother."

Nerites arched both eyebrows. "*Little prick?*"

Taking a step back, Prometheus motioned him in. "Yeah. He's made a habit on dropping in unannounced."

"Who has?" Nerites asked with a frown.

"Eros."

The frown deepened for a heartbeat, and then disappeared. "Father would like you to join his council meeting," he told Prometheus. "I trust you remember where the council room is. I heard you made an appearance recently."

So Nereus still planned to prepare for war. An all-out offense might work against Kronos, but it would destroy much of the human world. They'd need a contingency plan. If the witch could turn Prometheus back to stone lest he unravel, why couldn't she do the same for his unhinged brother? "Won't you join us?" he asked Nerites.

The prince of Vythos shook his head. "I've been briefed in advance, as per usual. Besides, I'm a lover, not a fighter. *Was*, anyway." Pain darkened his gaze so briefly, Prometheus wasn't sure he saw it.

Right. Nerites had been head over heels for Aphrodite. Her loss must have cost him dearly.

"Don't mention her," Pherusa warned in his head. To her brother, she said, "What about me?"

"You, my dear, can come fill our sisters in on your revived romance, before they drive me crazy with questions I have no answers to."

CHAPTER SEVENTEEN

Thirty of Pherusa's forty-nine sisters still lived at the palace, and most of them were gathered in the ball room. Large cushions were arranged in one side of the expansive room, and the Nereids were sprawled on them, oohing and ahing at all the right places, while Pherusa relayed a sex-free version of her reunion with her Titan.

Nerites stood beside a coral pillar in a corner, smiling at her, but Pherusa saw the sadness lurking in her brother's beautiful deep-blue eyes. Her one true love had been returned to her, while his was gone forever. The Titans wouldn't be waking if all the Olympians hadn't faded away, which meant all hope he had of winning Aphrodite's heart again was lost.

She tried to wrap up the remainder of her story and save him more torture, but the rest of the Nereids would have none of that.

"So he would destroy the entire world if the two of you didn't bond? That a whole new level of screwed up," Halie said. "And I thought ignoring Circe's prophecy came with dire consequences."

Pherusa rolled her eyes. "I know. And would you believe it? Before Prometheus came to accept I'd never hand him to Zeus, he was determined to go through with the unraveling. If it weren't for Eros' persistence, I wouldn't have found out, either, until it was too late."

Nerites' posture went as stiff as if a stingray had grazed him. "What did you say?"

Pherusa studied his furrowed brow. It didn't take away from the beauty of his face, though it aged him. "That I wouldn't know—"

He gestured impatiently. "No, before that."

"That Eros was the one who kept urging him to bond with me?"

"Yes." Nerites seemed confused. "Who is that?"

"Who's Eros?" Galene asked. "He's…" She shot Pherusa a panicked glance. They didn't mention Aphrodite's name in Nerite's presence when it could be avoided.

"The god of love," Pherusa supplied for her. No reason to remind her brother that Aphrodite had had a life after him, while he'd condemned himself to solitude.

Frowning, Nerites rubbed his temples. "How come I've never heard of him?"

Impossible. Nerites might have spent his entire life in Vythos, but you couldn't not have heard of Eros. "Perhaps you know him as Cupid?" Pherusa suggested.

He waved his hand in front of his face, as if to shoo away an annoying school of sardines. "Know whom as Cupid?"

For the second time, it was like Eros slipped her brother's mind. Or this was his way of letting them know he didn't want to hear about the god.

"Anyway, with some nudging, we performed the bonding." Pherusa let a naughty smile play on her lips. "A few times."

Halie laughed. "To make sure it took, of course." She was always quick to laugh since she and Delphinos bonded, and the sparkle of happiness suited her.

Pherusa knew the feeling of being so ecstatically blissful nothing could bring her down.

Except for her brother's lost expression.

"Are you done gossiping about me, ladies?" Prometheus' voice made her lift her gaze.

He leaned against the door frame, arms crossed over his wide chest, the seaweed struggling to contain his muscles. Imposing and regal in a dark-green robe wasn't an easy look to pull off, but he managed it impeccably.

Pherusa was on her feet and hurrying to him before she realized she moved.

"Hey! We didn't hear the juicy parts." Seemingly unperturbed by Prometheus' dirty look, Thalia added, "Whatever. Pherusa can fill us in later."

"How did the meeting go?" Pherusa asked when Prometheus whisked her out of the room. It was surreal, walking around her father's palace with her arm looped around her Titan's. So normal, and yet it had been out of her grasp even yesterday.

He nuzzled her hair. "As expected. We know Hyperion is awake, and according to Circe, he'll be on our side once he's bonded. Not that I'd ever expect him to join Kronos. Kronos has been quiet since you and I bonded"—he snorted—"for which your father congratulated me, though he wouldn't look me in the eye. We don't know how long this will last, so Nereus has patrols in all the seas, listening for signs of unusual activity."

Since the world was safe for now, Pherusa braved asking about matters closer to home. "And did everyone behave?" Through their mental link, she sent him, "Did you?"

His lips twitched. "There was some hero-worshiping, now that I didn't want to kill them. I got to know *your daimon friend* a little better too. He has a crush on you."

"You must be mistaken." Palaemon had been her escort to the surface since he was a young boy. She'd never seen him as more than a friend, and his behavior toward her betrayed no romantic feelings.

Prometheus shrugged. "Not like he told me he'll crush every bone in my body if I mistreat you. Twice."

"He *didn't*." She searched his thoughts. No hint of a lie. "You weren't uncivil to him, were you? I care about him deeply."

"And platonically, luckily for him and me both." Under the watchful gaze of two palace servants carrying linens, Prometheus brought her to a stop, folded an arm around her waist, and smashed his lips to hers in a kiss clearly meant to stake his claim. "Don't worry. I like the little guppy. He's loyal." He hummed and twirled her, before gathering her back in his embrace. "Was properly introduced to your sister's boy too. He's funny."

Pherusa laughed. If anyone would call hundreds-years-old sea daimons *guppy* and *boy*, it'd be Prometheus.

"What now?" she asked. "Can I have you to myself, or will you run off to play with your new friends?"

His gaze burned through her, the desire in his eyes making her feel as naked as ever. "I thought we'd stop by my cave first. Then, in a couple hours"—he waggled his eyebrows—"we could get dressed and go house shopping."

She licked her lips. "I hear house-shopping is best done in the afternoon, so we don't need to hurry."

"Then let's go to my cave and rut like beasts in heat."

CHAPTER EIGHTEEN

"One last signature here, and the place is yours." The realtor, Magda, tapped one red-lacquered nail on the dotted lines at the bottom of the contract, her red lips stretched in a shark-like grin.

Prometheus took the fountain pen she handed him, careful not to break it. *P. Titanas*, he scrawled. The deeds would be in his name only, because Pherusa didn't yet have any identification papers. He'd have to talk to Eros about those too. He'd seen the god's name in the contacts list of the cell phone Eros had given him.

Magda took the signed documents with a smile, sat back, and crossed her legs. She looked very pleased with herself, which made sense, since she'd no doubt be getting a hefty commission on the six-bedroom villa Prometheus and Pherusa bought.

Magda had shown them several houses in Santorini that were *almost* what they wanted, but the moment they set foot in that one, he and Pherusa both knew they had to have it. They fell in love with the ample space, the white walls carved into the stone, and the magnificent view of the Caldera. *And* it came furnished. It was the perfect home, and Prometheus looked forward to filling it with memories—and making love to his soulmate on every available surface.

Magda snapped her fingers, and her assistant, whose name Prometheus didn't remember, appeared at the door separating her office from the waiting room. "Yes, ma'am?"

His searing glower would put a Titan to shame, but Magda was unfazed. "Boy, get us a bottle of champagne. Mr. and Mrs. Titanas have gotten themselves the most gorgeous villa in all of Santorini, and we must celebrate it."

Pherusa glanced at Prometheus, a question in her eyes. "Champagne?" she asked.

He flipped through his new memories. Alcohol. Fizzy. *Nice.* "You'll like it." He patted her hand and looked at Magda. "Now what?" When he called to say they were serious about buying and would like everything done as soon as possible, she'd let him know Greek bureaucracy didn't do *as soon as possible*. "How long do we have to wait?"

She waved her hand dismissively. "Waiting is for those who can't afford to oil the wheels. Once the wire transfer comes through tomorrow, you may come get the keys. Spyros will make sure all the paperwork goes through by the end of the day."

Spyros. Right. Prometheus hadn't seen the young man on their two previous meetings with Magda, but he probably held the fort while boss-lady took clients on-site.

Spyros glared at her as he half-filled the flutes with the bubbly golden liquid. His eyes reminded Prometheus of someone, but he couldn't put his finger to it. Then again, Magda's eyes seemed familiar too. Maybe all blue eyes looked the same.

Magda tutted. "Only three glasses, boy. This is above your paygrade."

Prometheus brought his glass to his lips, to hide his amusement. There was something going on with these two.

"Not before we toast," Magda raised her glass, and he and Pherusa mimicked her. "To the newlyweds and their great taste. May you be happy together, always." She stressed the last word.

"Do you think he's... fucking her?" Pherusa stumbled over the f-word even in her thoughts.

Prometheus squinted against the fizz that threatened to come out of his nostrils. "If he is, he mustn't be doing a very good job of it," he replied through their link. He stood and held out his hand to Magda. "Thank you so much for your help."

"You've made a wonderful choice," Spyros said. The way his gaze strayed to Pherusa, Prometheus wasn't sure he meant the villa, but he wouldn't go primitive on the boy's ass. Only a blind man wouldn't be awed by her.

Magda shook hands with him and Pherusa, and then said, "Spyros will show you out. Drop by tomorrow around noon for the keys."

"We have a house." Pherusa clapped and planted a noisy kiss on Prometheus' mouth when the realtor's door closed behind them. "I can't believe we can move in tomorrow."

He brushed a lock of hair back from her face and winked. "We'll have the keys tomorrow. No reason to wait till then to move in." He closed his arms around her, cast a wide mental net over onlookers, so their gazes would glide off him and his Siren, and blinked with her to their new bedroom.

EPILOGUE

"Are they gone, *boy*?" Circe shouldn't be enjoying this charade so much, but Eros' discomfort at his role as assistant to her bitch-realtor persona was hilarious.

"You'd better be waiting for me naked," he hollered from the next room. He strode in her—well, *Magda's*, if she were to be technical about it—office and slammed the door behind him, his true facial features taking over the magic disguise. "*Boy?* You'll be lucky to only get away with a spanking."

"Oh, did I upset you, baby?" She batted her eyelashes, letting the realtor's pale skin deepen to her own golden tan, and the blond pixie cut give way to her chestnut locks. She might be kinky, but Eros' having sex with Magda's lookalike would be the wrong kind of *bad*.

"How long do we have?" he asked.

Circe looked at the clock hanging beside the door. "It's an hour and a half by car. Two, if they hit traffic. And that's after she decides he's a no-show." She'd intercepted Prometheus' last call and had sent the actual realtor, who had no assistant, to meet a nonexistent client in Nafplio, so she and Eros could make sure Prometheus and Pherusa got the perfect place with no legal hassle. Magda might not remember closing the deal, but she wouldn't mind getting the commission.

"Why couldn't we tell the big guy we were doing him a favor, intercepting for the realtor?" Eros grasped her skirt with both hands and pulled it higher, to expose her bare ass.

"Because this is more fun." And because Circe's visions told her to do so. If she hadn't reached into Magda's mind, to view her previous meetings with Prometheus and Pherusa, she wouldn't have recognized the latent—

Eros popped open the buttons of her pressed white shirt and dug his teeth in her flesh. "Where are you?" he asked.

She moaned and pulled at his hair, but they both knew she enjoyed a little pain.

"Right here, with you, my..." Instead of finishing that sentence, she flicked her tongue along the seam of his mouth, and bit his bottom lip when he pulled away.

"You and your secrets and your games..." With a wild laugh, Eros turned her and bent her over Magda's desk. "Now you've done it." His palm landed on her bare bottom with a loud *smack*.

Circe pushed all thoughts of Magda's reborn soul out of her mind. It wasn't *her* time yet, anyway.

THE END

But keep reading for a sneak peek into Titans #2, *A Maid for the Titan*

When Zeus abandoned Olympus, Hyperion was sure he'd be left behind, but that wouldn't be punishment enough. From one conscious moment to the next, he no longer stood on green grass, but was surrounded by dark, still waters. He gave up. Stopped trying to see or hear. No light reached the depths of the sea that was to be his grave.

Then one day he awoke, and he was in this room, surrounded by noise and humans and lights. Voices spoke in tongues that made no sense, and a large opening on the wall across from him showed him images of war and famine and celebration. Of love and hate. After ages of feeling only cold, now warmth caressed his bare back for a while every few... hours? He chose to believe it was Helios, heralding the morning and shining down on him. Reminding him he wasn't alone.

But wasn't he? His brothers were lost to him, and the females of his generation were long gone. Hyperion couldn't begrudge his nephew the safety precautions. He'd warned Kronos not to eat his children, lest he share Uranus' fate, but did the giant pain in the glutes listen? No. And all Titans paid for it.

Hyperion didn't care whether the mortals that came and went were friends or foes; he could best any human. He yelled inside his head and raged against the unseen shackles holding him immobile. But Zeus' spell had enough of a hold over him that the void never failed to suck him back in.

Something brushed along his manhood and pulled him out of his spiraling thoughts. That he could feel it wasn't surprising. He hadn't lost sensation when he was turned into stone.

What *was* surprising was that he physically responded to the stimulus. The touch was feather light, but his body rose to the occasion.

Huh? His body had been locked in position for eons, and the one part that decided to move after all this time was what hung between his legs?

He looked down—*he looked down?*—and saw a dark-haired woman staring up, under his loincloth, her brown eyes wide and her lips parted. It had been a very long while since a woman looked at him with such open interest, let alone evoked a response.

The woman licked her lips, and his manhood grew to its fully erect position, which couldn't possibly fit inside a mortal female. Was this a new kind of torture—getting him ready to enter a female's body and leaving him incapable of sating his hunger? Another of Zeus' tricks? Hyperion groaned, and the woman gave a little jump and spun around.

No. She'd leave, and he'd be stuck here like a satyr, with desire burning in his loins.

He ached for her to finish what she started. He didn't realize when his hand moved, but he was no longer holding the ceiling. Delighted, he cupped himself. *Yes.* He could feel his palm on his shaft. Could feel the fabric between his grip and his erection. Was he turning into flesh again? Was his unjust punishment finally over?

*

Need more? Get Hyperion and Olivia's story now!

ABOUT THE AUTHOR

Sotia shares her life and living quarters with her husband, their son, and two rescue dogs, one of which may be part-pony. Sappy movies make her cry, and she wishes she could take in all the stray dogs in the world.

Sotia spent her formative years reading anything she could get her hands on, including steamy romances her grandma would frown upon—nah, Grandma would totally approve.

Hailing from the land of Olympians and Titans, Sotia could only resist writing about mythical immortals for so long. Her mythology romance boasts hot, powerful Alphas, who can handle sassy ladies and will stop at nothing to make them happy.

True love exists, and Sotia is determined to give her fated couples a happy ending!

*

To know more about Sotia, get your hands on freebies, and be the first to hear about new releases, check out her website!

www.sotialazu.com

www.ingramcontent.com/pod-product-compliance
Lightning Source LLC
Chambersburg PA
CBHW071005120726
47910CB00004B/1392